"The sky's amaz

She felt a tickle against her skin. "I know. It's as ~~lovely~~
music."

"I'm looking at something even lovelier."

She lowered her gaze.

"I'm talking about you, Juli."

In the dark she could hide her blush. She couldn't remember being told she was lovely by anyone, except maybe
her mother. "Thanks, but—"

"No buts. Please accept the compliment."

She could only nod and cling to the compliment as if it
were a treasure. "This has been a great evening."

"I'm glad you took another chance on—"

She pressed her finger against his lips to silence him, and
he kissed it. She drew her hand away, feeling the tingle of his
touch. "We'll forget that first date. Let's pretend this is our
first."

"I like that idea." He drew her closer. "We'll do this again,
and soon."

She sent him a smile as big as the one in her heart. "I'd
love to."

"But this time it'll be different. I don't like your driving
alone at night. I'll pick you up."

"No. Please. I don't mind—"

This time his finger covered her lips. "Let me be a gentleman. I want to pick you up. We can do something in your area."

Like smell the garlic. Her spirit slumped. One day he'd
have to visit her home and family. *Lord, help me get over this
weirdness.*

GAIL GAYMER MARTIN says that when friends tell her about funny, frightening, or poignant events in their lives, they sometimes stop short and ask, "Will you write about this in your next novel?" Gail only smiles. Sometimes she does, but with a twist. Gail feels awed to write stories that honor the Lord and touch people's hearts. With forty contracted books, Gail is a multi-award-winning author published in fiction and nonfiction. Her novels have received numerous national awards, and she has more than a million books in print.

Gail, a cofounder of American Christian Fiction Writers, lives in Michigan with her husband, Bob. When not behind her computer, she enjoys a busy life—traveling, presenting workshops at conferences, speaking at churches and libraries, and singing as a soloist and member of her church choir, in which she also plays handbells and handchimes. She is also a member of one of the finest Christian chorales in Michigan, the Detroit Lutheran Singers.

Visit her Web site at www.gailmartin.com and visit her blog site at www.gailmartin.blogspot.com. Write to Gail at PO Box 760063, Lathrup Village, MI, 48076 or at authorgailmartin@aol.com. She enjoys hearing from readers.

Books by Gail Gaymer Martin

HEARTSONG PRESENTS
HP302—Seasons
HP330—Dreaming of Castles
HP462—Secrets Within
HP489—Over Her Head
HP594—Out on a Limb
HP770—And Baby Makes Five

Don't miss out on any of our super romances. Write to us at the following address for information on our newest releases and club information.

Heartsong Presents Readers' Service
PO Box 721
Uhrichsville, OH 44683

Or visit www.heartsongpresents.com

Garlic and Roses

Gail Gaymer Martin

Heartsong Presents

To Bob, who makes everything fall into place when things seem to be falling apart. A husband who brings me bouquets just because he loves me.

A note from the Author:
I love to hear from my readers! You may correspond with me by writing:

Gail Gaymer Martin
Author Relations
PO Box 721
Uhrichsville, OH 44683

ISBN 978-1-59789-931-4

GARLIC AND ROSES

Scripture quotations are taken from the King James Version of the Bible.

Scripture quotations also taken from the HOLY BIBLE, NEW INTERNATIONAL VERSION ®. NIV ®. Copyright © 1973, 1978, 1984 by International Bible Society. Used by permission of Zondervan. All rights reserved.

All of the characters and events in this book are fictitious. Any resemblance to actual persons, living or dead, or to actual events is purely coincidental.

Our mission is to publish and distribute inspirational products offering exceptional value and biblical encouragement to the masses.

PRINTED IN THE U.S.A.

one

"Will that be all?" Juliana Maretti asked from behind the checkout counter, her eye on the clock. She smiled at the couple gazing around the store, their mouths agape. The camera around the gentleman's neck validated her guess that they were tourists.

"What about those braided garlic bunches?" The woman pointed to the display. "How long will they last?"

"Months. Just let them hang in a dry place. Don't refrigerate them."

The woman studied the display for a moment then turned back to Juli. "We'll take one of those." She motioned to her husband, who headed for the display and brought a braid back to the counter.

She took it from him and held it in the air, tilting her head like a woman deciding which dress to purchase.

Juli managed not to tap her fingernails against the counter. She had paperwork to do and some orders to check before she could leave.

"Maybe we should buy two," the woman said, turning to her husband. "Do you think Mama would like one? She uses a lot of garlic in her cooking." She turned from her husband back to Juli. "She's Italian."

"So am I." Juli nodded then glanced at her watch again, wondering how much longer before she could get on with her work. That was the problem of managing a store. When an ailing clerk left, the manager took over until a replacement arrived. "Italians like their garlic, but then, so do many people." She motioned in a wide span toward the products filling the store. "We sell many garlic products—useful items and

5

gourmet foods. I'm sure your mother will enjoy a practical gift like the braid."

The woman gestured toward the display, and her husband stepped across the aisle to grab another one while Juli totaled the sale. She bagged the produce, made change, and thanked them as they stepped away.

Some days seemed to drag on endlessly. Juli wondered what it would be like to love a job so much that the time flew. If she had a dream, that would be it. She eyed her watch again and released a sigh. Two hours to go and she still had her own work to do, and today she needed to leave early. She turned toward the door. Donna had promised to come in as soon as she could. So where was she?

Customers ambled through her father's store. The Garlic Garden brought in many customers each day, especially in the summer when tourists visited Gilroy.

"Juliana."

Juli turned toward the voice and eyed the woman's face, which looked uncomfortably familiar. "Can I help you?" She scrutinized the features, realizing she should know her.

"You don't remember me?"

The woman moved closer, and beneath the makeup and salon-induced blond hair, Juli recognized her, a girl from her graduating class. "Melanie."

"How could you forget?"

The barb in her voice dug deep. Juli ignored the question. "How are you?"

"Great." Her gaze did a slow scan of her father's store. "I see you're the same."

Another dig. "I'm glad you're doing well. What brings you here?"

"A sorority friend from out of town. She wanted to see the infamous garlic kingdom." Her lilting laugh had a biting edge as she waved across the room to an attractive young woman browsing through the garlic sauces.

Sorority friend. Juli not only had no sorority sister, but she had never gone to college. Instead she'd stayed home to manage her father's store, and her brother had earned his degree. Her father's old-world attitude butted against Juli's, but she believed in honoring her father and mother. The memory knifed her once again, leaving a reopened wound. "Nice of you to show her the town."

Juli peered at the growing line at the checkout. She looked over her shoulder. "Sandra, would you give Donna another call, please?" She eyed Melanie and motioned toward the customers. "Sorry. I need to wait on these people."

Melanie arched her eyebrow and shifted away.

Juli waited on the next customer while battling her desire to check on Melanie and her friend. Melanie had brought back bad memories of her senior year when she and Juli were both running for Gilroy High Garlic Queen. The incident pried out memories that hurt, and Juli struggled to push them from her mind.

"Thank you," she said, handing the customer his change.

The man smiled and moved off while she waited on another. When she'd finished, Melanie's overly friendly voice penetrated her thoughts. "Roxy, this is Juliana, the one I told you about."

Roxy eyed Juli and snickered. "You mean the garlic and roses bouquet?"

Melanie sent her a look as if warning her not to say any more, but the damage had been done. Juli knew the bouquet had been a mean prank played on her long ago, and she suspected Melanie had been behind the incident even though she came through it unscathed.

Juli managed to grin. "Yes. Garlic and roses. It was unique." Juli tried to keep her voice lighthearted. "Will this be it?"

"That's it." Roxy dug into her handbag while Juli rang up the items.

She ran the credit card and returned it to the woman along

with her purchases. "I hope you enjoy your visit."

"It's been fun, but I don't know how you can live with this smell."

"Ask Melanie. She's apparently still in the area. It grows on you." Juli watched a flash of anger in Melanie's eyes and wanted to chalk up one notch for herself, but she knew it was wrong to hurt people. As the two women walked away, Juli looked heavenward, asking God to forgive her dig to Melanie. She knew better than to let the old situation get under her skin again.

Back in high school she and Melanie had been nominated for Gilroy High Garlic Queen in their senior year. Besides being queen of the senior events, the honor included participating in the garlic festival at the end of July. Melanie's competition with Juli had been fierce, and Juli never understood why. Melanie was pretty and very popular with okay grades. Though Juli had good grades, she wasn't popular. In fact, the popular kids considered her a nerd. While Melanie's father had a lucrative business, Juli's father's business had just become so, and the businesses were different. Juli had struggled with the question of how she'd even been nominated until she thought she'd finally learned the answer.

She let her thoughts dwindle and concentrated on the customers, and after Donna arrived, Juli focused on her paperwork and checked the orders. When the hour hand finally moved to four, Juli gave final instructions to her replacement manager, said good-bye to her coworkers, and scooted out the door. The drive to Seaside near Monterey would take her awhile in the heavy traffic, and she liked to arrive at the soup kitchen on time even if it was only a volunteer job.

❧

Juli found a parking spot behind the building and dug into her shoulder bag for a scrunchie. She pulled the soft fabric-covered elastic from the bottom of her bag and tied her hair into a ponytail. After locking the car, she hurried into the back door of the soup kitchen, knowing she had arrived late.

A mixture of smells met her at the door: tomatoes, beef, and the familiar scent of garlic. She eyed a large pot of beef and tomatoes stewing on the burner, elbow macaroni bubbling on another burner—goulash, she noted—and bowls of peaches lined up on trays.

"Sorry," Juli said, waving to a couple of volunteers she knew. "You know the traffic."

She darted past them to the storage area, stuffed her purse inside, and tied on the standard bib apron then checked the task chart. Her assignment: cookies. On the way to her station, Juli grabbed a pair of the plastic gloves sitting everywhere in boxes. One thing the soup kitchen demanded was cleanliness. She pulled out a carton of chocolate chip cookies and tugged on the stubborn lid.

"Juli."

She looked up as Bill Montego stepped to her side.

He tilted his head toward the dining room. "We have a big crowd waiting outside. It looks like we'll have a passel of people tonight. The doors open in twenty minutes."

"I'm on it," she said, pulling the carton closer, determined to pry open the lid without help.

Bill beckoned to someone behind her. "This is Alan, a new volunteer. Could you show him the ropes?"

"Sure thing." She glanced over her shoulder and looked into the most beautiful dusky lilac-blue eyes she'd ever seen.

"I hope you don't mind," Alan said. "What can I do to help?" He motioned to the carton she'd been trying to open.

"Glad you've decided to join us. We can always use help." She stopped attacking the lid. "I'm Juli Maretti." She nodded toward the gloves lying beside her. "You need to be sterilized." She grinned and pointed to the glove box. "You can get yours over there."

He followed her directions and strode to the box of gloves.

When he turned back, he waved them in the air, his warm smile sparkling. "I'm Alan Louden, by the way. If you're my boss, we need to be properly introduced."

She loved his lightheartedness. Realizing she was fighting an unending battle, she slid the carton in front of him. "Maybe you can do this."

He pried the lid open in the blink of an eye then slipped his hands into plastic gloves. Together they began unpacking the cookies and setting them onto trays.

In the monotony of the task, she wanted to talk, but she felt tongue-tied as she so often did when it came to socializing with men her age. Her dating experience had been basically nil.

Alan grasped a handful of cookies and paused. "How long have you been volunteering here?"

His voice broke through the silence and surprised her. "A year or more," she said, wishing she didn't feel so jumpy when she looked into his gorgeous eyes and friendly smile.

He removed the filled tray and replaced it with an empty one. "Are you from Seaside?"

She hated to say she was from Gilroy. It was the same old line—"You live in the garlic capital of the world" or some such comment. She couldn't bear any more Gilroy jokes. "A friend of mine lives in Monterey and dragged me here to be her moral support. Then she quit coming, but I was hooked."

"Good for you." His smile radiated to her heart. "Too many people take their good fortune for granted."

She liked the sound of his voice—a rich baritone with a hint of good humor. Most of all she liked what he'd just said. "You're right. People grumble about so many things when they have so much. Spending a few days in a soup kitchen would be a lesson in being thankful."

He patted her arm. "I like you," he said. "You're smart." He lifted the same hand with a chuckle. "But I'm not." He peeled off the plastic glove and reached into the box for a fresh one.

She chuckled at his blunder. "I think most of the volunteers here agree with you. They're giving from the heart."

He gave her a concurring nod and dug back into the carton for more cookies.

By the time they'd filled the trays, Bill flagged them into the dining room to help serve. As Juli dished out food, she thought about Bill's asking her to train Alan. He could have asked so many others, but he'd asked her, and it pleased Juli. She liked volunteering, and she liked Alan. Juli's work at the soup kitchen was fulfilling, and the time flew by, the way she wished her real job did.

Pulling her mind free, Juli concentrated on serving those in line. The next woman holding out her tray was one of Juli's favorites, and she sent the woman a smile. "How are you?"

The older woman shrugged with sad eyes. "Not so good today."

Juli noticed how worn and tired she looked and made a mental note to speak with her later. She made it a point to talk with those who appeared to need someone to listen.

Alan shifted beside her. "You seem to know a lot of these people."

Juli nodded. "They come back week after week. Sometimes it's hard to remember they may be down and out, but they're people just like you and me." She turned to face him and saw the seriousness in his eyes. "There but for the grace of God go I. I think of that phrase every time I work here. God's been good to my family, but it's due to His grace and nothing more."

Alan's expression darkened.

She searched his eyes for a moment, wondering if maybe he didn't believe in the Lord. Being a Christian wasn't a prerequisite for volunteering, but many of the volunteers were believers.

With the question niggling her, she focused on the line, trying to smile and talk with the homeless men and women she'd seen there so often, but despite her efforts her mind tangled with thoughts about Alan. When he wasn't on her mind, she thought back to her edgy meeting with Melanie earlier in the day. Why had Melanie found it necessary to mention the garlic and rose bouquet? That had been so hurtful, and yet what did it matter now? At the time she'd thought she had been the brunt of a class joke when the school voted her the Gilroy High Garlic Queen. The honor always went to the most beautiful and most popular. Melanie was popular and should have won hands down.

But after the event she'd learned the truth. She'd won mainly because of the underclassmen. They were apparently tired of Melanie's belittling comments. But still, something else had happened. Juli could only guess that when Melanie suspected she wouldn't win, she'd had her friends vote for Juli, too, to ensure she became the garlic queen so they could make a joke out of the situation. Juli recalled this had happened another time before she entered high school. Teenagers could be terribly mean at times.

"You just put goulash on top of her salad." Alan's voice jolted her.

Juli looked at the woman's plate and released a sigh. "Sorry." She reached out and took the dish, returned to the food stations, and refilled the woman's choices, adding a little extra to make up for her absentmindedness.

When she returned the plate, the woman eyed the portion and gave her a broad, missing-tooth smile. "Thank you," she said.

Juli grinned back. "You're welcome."

From her expression Juli guessed the woman hoped she would make the same mistake next week.

Alan leaned closer. "That was a kind thing you did. She'll remember that always."

"The goulash on her salad?"

His eyes looked unexpectedly serious. "You know what I mean."

Though she wondered about his comment, she grasped the

ladle and doled out the goulash, forcing her mind to stick to her work.

a

As the crowd wandered back outside, Alan invited those left to have seconds, but he couldn't keep Juli from his mind. He'd been watching her stop to speak with some of the diners. He could tell she wasn't patronizing. She really listened to them, even patting their hands and giving a few hugs. He hadn't recalled ever seeing that kind of personal attention given at soup kitchens, and Juli's action touched him. When the people left, they seemed to be holding their heads higher and walking with a lighter step. Alan wanted to listen to what she said and learn from her example.

After leaving the serving counter, Juli had untied her ponytail, and now her dark curly hair hung in long kinks a little below her shoulders. He loved the wispy ends that seemed to have a mind of their own. He wondered if Juli had the same kind of stubborn independence. Her deep brown eyes flashed as she talked, and her warm smile tugged at his heart.

Alan glanced at his watch. Weariness had settled over him. He'd worked a twelve-hour day at the hospital, and standing on his feet the past three hours had added stress to his already aching back. Since the hall held only a few last-minute diners, he knew he could leave, but lifting his shoulders for a second breath, he devised a plan. Instead of slipping away, he rolled out the trash can to help clear the tables and wipe them down.

While cleaning tables, Alan studied Juli as she gave a tender pat to another homeless man who rose to leave. Alan waited until the man had stepped away before he pulled the trash can closer to her and stopped. "You amaze me."

Her eyes widened. "Really?"

"You do."

The wide-eyed look changed to a curious frown. "Why?"

Alan gestured toward the last people walking through the door. "You're so...so relaxed with these people even though so many are scraggy-looking. You seem to send them away with something special."

"Food for the stomach and food for the soul. I send them away with hope."

"Hope?" The word sank into his thoughts. These people needed so many things, and hope was definitely one of them. "That's a good thing."

"Especially for the people who have so little. Have you ever listened to their stories?"

He'd known only one story—his own. "No."

"Next time talk to them and listen. Anyone with compassion, and I think you have it, will want to do whatever they can to lift their spirits."

Guilt gnawed at Alan's usually well-fed stomach. Though he'd often been able to show he had compassion for the sick, he hadn't extended it here today and had the same problem at the hospital. "I will."

She joined him in tossing paper plates and napkins into the trash. "These people aren't all druggies and drunks. Some of them have other problems—serious family situations and no place to turn."

Alan nodded, knowing the truth in her statement. Juli had captured his interest. Whether it was her spirit, her faith that seemed so evident, or the good humor he'd seen, he wasn't sure, but he wanted to know her better.

He left her filling the trash can and went into the kitchen for a bucket of water and a cloth to wipe down the tables. Other workers were packing leftovers and cleaning the kitchen while some were pushing large brooms along the floor. People pitched in, he noticed. Nothing was too lowly for any of them. Good hearts, he thought.

Alan wiped down the final table, scanned the room, and dropped the cloth into the bucket then headed to the kitchen storage closet. When he disposed of the equipment, he turned and saw Juli draping her purse over her shoulder. "Looks like we're finished," he said.

"We had a big crowd tonight. Usually we're done sooner." She took a few steps then stopped. "By the way, it was nice meeting you."

Alan felt his stomach rumble as he searched her eyes. "Do you have time for coffee? I noticed a diner up the road."

She looked at her watch then lifted her tired eyes to his. "I'd love to, but it's getting late, and I have a long drive home."

He felt deflated. "I understand. Maybe another time." He stuck out his hand. "Thanks for showing me around tonight. I appreciate it."

"You're welcome," she said, grasping his hand in an amiable shake.

Her hand felt small in his, and the warmth rolled up his arm. He wished she had agreed to stop for coffee. His disappointment multiplied that she hadn't said maybe next time. Despite his letdown, he wouldn't give up. Trying to get to know someone here would be difficult. They had little time to talk about important things.

"I'll walk you out." He pulled the apron over his head and hung it on a hook.

"Thanks."

She moved into step with him, and he pushed open the door to the pleasant spring air.

Juli pointed. "I'm parked over there."

He walked beside her, wanting to talk but not knowing what to say.

When she stopped beside a small sedan, he finally found his voice. "I hope I'll see you next week."

"You'll be back?"

He heard the quiet beep when she hit the remote. "I want to spread a little of that hope you're so good at sharing."

"That's great," she said, opening the car door. She paused

a moment then turned toward him. "By the way, Saturday is 'Dining Out, Helping Out' day. Some of the volunteers meet at Crazy Horse Restaurant to support the Monterey Food Bank. The restaurant's in the Park Hotel."

"I know the place."

Her eyes brightened. "Good, and 10 percent of the profits go to help the hungry, in case you didn't know."

"I know about the charity. A number of restaurants in the area donate some of their proceeds."

She nodded. "I've been to Big Joe's in Salinas. It's closer to me, but since this is central for the volunteers, we usually meet in Monterey." She sent him an amazing smile. "I'll be there about six. Come, and we can talk then. If not, I'll see you next Wednesday."

"I'll check my calendar." Her smile warmed him, and he hoped he could see her Saturday. He watched her settle into the car and start the engine before he dragged himself away, hungry and tired but feeling uplifted.

⁂

Juli tried to keep up with the conversation at the Crazy Horse Restaurant. She'd been certain Alan would show up. Wondering why he hadn't come, she only half listened to the conversation, trying to laugh at the right times and respond when it was appropriate.

The waiting rattled her. It seemed too much like her youth when she waited for someone to ask her to the sophomore party or the junior dinner. When she'd about given up waiting to be asked, someone—usually someone who'd been refused by numerous others—finally appeared with an invitation. By then she wanted to say no, but she'd always been taught not to "cut off her nose to spite her face," so she accepted the date.

She had some friends but no real boyfriends—just pals. She knew why. She'd never been allowed to wear jeans and the revealing tops the girls wore. Her dad insisted she wear loose-fitting clothing and sturdy shoes. She felt as if she'd come over from Italy in steerage rather than being a modern-day teen. He thought he was following God's Word and reminded her of 1 Peter 3:3: "Whose adorning let it not be that outward adorning of plaiting the hair, and of wearing of gold, or of putting on of apparel." He stressed modesty, but she felt so out of place in school. That was seven years ago, though. *Let it go, Juli.*

"What's happening?"

Juli turned and looked into a pair of brown eyes. "Nothing much." She'd seen the new volunteer before, but his name escaped her.

"Your watch seems better company than we are."

She clasped her palm over her watch and slipped her hands to her lap. "Sorry. I have a long drive home." She cringed hearing her comment. It was the truth, but it had nothing to do with her checking the time.

He gave her a little nudge. "Waiting for someone?"

She realized he was flirting with her, and she tried to smile. "A friend mentioned stopping by. We didn't set real plans."

"Good," he said, sliding his chair closer. "Did anyone ever tell you that you have a great smile?"

Here he goes. She shrugged, trying to find a good way to respond. "My dentist."

His expectant look opened to laughter. "That's a great one. I'll have to remember that."

She pulled her hands from beneath the table, taking another moment to glance at her watch.

He leaned in. "I've noticed you on Wednesdays. I love your hair and your smile, but you're quiet. You seem all business. You sort of give people the cold shoulder."

You seem all business. The cold shoulder. A light went on in Juli's head. Had she chased away young men with her quiet, businesslike way? Maybe she seemed aloof. She knew that could be a defense mechanism to avoid rejection. The possibility startled her. "The soup kitchen is serious business.

I try to focus on the people who need help. It's what I feel is important."

His hand moved closer to hers, and he brushed the back of it with his finger. "I'm not criticizing. Focusing on people is a worthy purpose."

She looked at him, wondering if he was being sincere or just flirting.

"I choose to focus on you, Juli." He gave her a wink.

That answered her question. She felt uncomfortable with the man and even more not knowing his name. "Sorry, but I don't know your name."

He brushed his finger against her arm. "I know yours."

"I know mine, too." She grinned, surprised the comment gave her a chuckle. "But I don't know yours."

"Dill. Short for Dillon."

She extended her hand. "Dill it is. I like to know the volunteers."

"I'd like to know you." He took her hand and didn't let go.

Trying to ease her fingers from his, an uneasy sensation rolled over her. She turned in time to see Alan with his back to the dining room heading toward the exit. Before she could move, he'd disappeared.

"Excuse me a minute," she said, jerking her hand from Dill's and bolting toward the exit.

When she stepped outside, she looked both ways, but Alan had vanished. She closed her eyes, trying to fathom if he had seen Dill holding her hand. If so, what had he thought?

two

Alan removed his scrubs and pulled on his jeans then tugged his polo shirt over his head. The day had been difficult following a bad car accident on Fremont Boulevard, and he was glad to leave the stress behind him. His thoughts stressed him, too. He kept picturing Juli holding some guy's hand at the restaurant.

Before the restaurant incident, Juli had filled his thoughts in a wonderful way. Now he felt confused. He looked forward to seeing her again so he could make sense out of the hand-holding circumstances. He'd hoped this time she would stop afterward for coffee. He'd thought about her relationship with the homeless, the way she seemed to befriend them, and he wished he could be a little mouse, listening to what she said to them. It had definitely made a difference. Though he spent his career working in the emergency room, he'd faced the sad fact that he didn't have the knack of comforting people in that situation, either. He worked to save lives but forgot about the whole person sometimes.

Alan dropped his scrubs into a duffle bag and swung through the doorway, whacking the bag against something solid.

"Whoa!" Tom Denny staggered back then arched his brows. "Where are you headed in such a hurry?"

Embarrassed at his preoccupation, Alan found his voice. "I volunteer at a soup kitchen on Wednesdays. Want to come along?" Though he'd asked the question, he counted on Tom's saying no.

"Since when do they take care of medical needs at a soup kitchen?"

Alan chuckled. "This isn't medical. It's soup."

Tom curled up his nose. "You ladle soup?"

"Last week I ladled goulash." The picture of Juli dumping goulash on the woman's salad made him grin.

Tom's frown deepened. "Why?"

The question caught Alan in the chest. He'd kept his personal life to himself, and he planned to continue keeping it private. "It's a good thing to do. Our focus at the hospital is good health, but without nourishment people can't have good health. The two go hand in hand." An uneasy truth skittered up his back. Juli had become another motivation.

Tom shrugged. "I suppose you're right."

"As always, Nurse Denny"— he gave Tom a grin—"you should know that for certain. Food and health were taught in Medicine 101."

He chuckled and shook his head. "You got me, Alan."

Alan gave Tom's arm a shake. "Now you know why I volunteer." He took a step away before Tom spoke again.

Tom crinkled his nose. "I suppose the volunteers are a bunch of old folks."

"Old? Not really. I've met some nice people of all ages."

"All ages?" Tom searched Alan's eyes a moment before continuing.

The question singed Alan's patience. "I don't ask to see their drivers' licenses."

Tom chuckled. "If there's a young crowd, maybe I'll go with you next week. I'd like to meet some new people. Where is the place?"

Though he was pleased Tom wanted to volunteer, the motivation irked him. Alan harnessed his irritation. "In Seaside."

"I'll think about it." Tom opened his locker.

"I need to get moving. I'll see you tomorrow." Alan turned away, and this time he kept going, wanting to kick himself for inviting Tom and feeling guilty that he wanted to discourage him from volunteering. The charity always needed help, but Tom was a charmer. He worried Tom might come on to the women—Juli in particular.

A sigh sneaked from him. He'd wanted Juli all for himself, and Tom was another good-looking bachelor like that dude at the restaurant. Tom had his choice of a number of lovely young nurses at the hospital, and he'd dated many of them. Alan, on the other hand, didn't have Tom's gift of gab, but more than that he wasn't comfortable with Tom's flitting from one woman to the next. If Alan was looking for a relationship, he would want one with some real depth that might lead to a commitment. Tom's values and his didn't mesh.

If Tom really wanted to volunteer, another problem centered in Alan's mind. He'd been quiet about his career at the charity, and he feared Tom might let everyone know. The last thing Alan wanted was a fuss about his being a physician. He wanted to participate by affecting lives in a different way, a way that meant too much to him. The need was great, and more hands made the work easier. His mother had often said something like that to him when he was a kid.

His mother. Every time he thought of her, he ached inside. Talk about a difficult life—his mother had been a prime example. Widowed with five small children and no work skills, she'd done everything to keep the family together, and Alan would always be grateful. Though he remembered the bad times, the rough edges were smoothed by what he had learned about survival and about the Lord.

Juli had mentioned God, and he wondered if it had been just a phrase—"there but for the grace of God go I"—or if it really reflected her relationship with the Lord.

He shook his head. *Stop guessing.* He felt like a kid who'd experienced his first heart flutter over a girl. He'd looked forward to seeing Juli again, but after seeing her with the other man on Saturday, confusion put him on edge.

What would he do when he saw her tonight. . .if he saw her

tonight? Act normal, that's all he could do, and if she didn't mention the restaurant, neither would he. It would be easier.

৯

Juli stirred the pasta, her attention more on the door than the noodles. Alan had said he'd be there again this week, and she'd expected him to follow through. Then something had happened at the restaurant. She could only guess he'd seen her with Dill and made an assumption. She felt awful. Dill was a flirt with no serious purpose in mind. And something about Alan made her feel comfortable, as if she'd known him for years. Maybe it was the kindness in his eyes. His eyes. She could picture the twinkle behind the dusky lilac-blue that reminded her of rain clouds with a glimmer of sun shining through.

After she'd pulled away the week before, she wished she'd accepted Alan's invitation for coffee. They would have gotten to know each other better, and he wouldn't have reached the wrong conclusion at the restaurant. It had been late, but so what? Once again she knew why she'd hesitated. He would ask her more about herself, and she hated to talk about her life. Garlic. Why hadn't she outgrown that problem? Her father had been a garlic farmer since she'd been born. Just before she entered high school, he'd bought the building for a store, and now it was well known. Her father's hard work had grown into a lucrative business and given her many advantages. She should be proud rather than uncomfortable, and he'd changed, too, through the years. He'd softened.

But the taunts in high school still rang in her ears. Garlic Breath. Garlic Bud. Garlic Clove. Garlic Head. She'd heard them all from Melanie's friends. They all lived in Gilroy. If they disliked garlic so much, why didn't their families move away? Her shoulders tightened with the memories.

"Hi."

Juli jumped, and a few macaroni noodles flew from the spoon.

"Sorry," she said, amazed at how fast Alan had ducked from being splattered with the pasta elbows.

He bent down and picked up the mess from the floor. "I didn't realize you had a weapon in your hand."

She managed a grin while her cheeks burned with embarrassment. "Next time it might be more than buckshot."

"Noodle shot, you mean." He strode to the trash can and dropped the pasta inside then eyed the stove. "Same as last week? Is it goulash every Wednesday?"

"Macaroni and cheese tonight." She motioned with her free hand to the large pans of melting cheese.

"I love that stuff. Maybe I'll go outside and get in line."

Playing, she arched her brow. "I'd recommend you get to work."

"What's my job?"

"I think that's your station." She pointed to the salad area. "They're shorthanded." She'd peeked at the task chart to see where he would be.

He turned and eyed the salad station. "Is there a place to double check?"

"The task chart is on the wall near the door." With his eyes he followed the direction in which she pointed then turned and walked across the kitchen to check the list.

After seeing him leave the restaurant on Saturday, Juli couldn't believe how natural and friendly he seemed. Had she been mistaken? Maybe the person she saw leaving wasn't Alan at all but someone who looked like him.

Alan returned, looking amused. "You were right."

She felt compelled to be truthful. "I checked earlier."

"Thanks. It's nice to know you care." He scanned the kitchen then gave her a questioning look.

She guessed he was looking for Dill and decided to ask. "What happened on Saturday?"

Alan looked uneasy. "Saturday. I—I—"

"Was it you I saw leaving? I ran outside, but you'd vanished.

All I could think was it was someone who looked just like you." She could see the answer in his eyes.

"It was me. I'm sorry. I just—"

She knew the answer, but she wanted to hear it from him. "Did you see me with that guy?"

He lowered his head. "Yes. I didn't feel comfortable, and I didn't want to interrupt."

"Interrupt what? He was coming on to me." Her pulse galloped. "I was waiting for you to save me."

His eyebrows lifted. "Save you? Really?"

Heat rose up her neck. "Really."

Alan drew closer and touched her arm. "Juli, I'm so sorry. You were holding hands, and I thought I'd misunderstood your invitation. I assumed you'd met someone, and. . . My showing up with an idea of spending time with you would have been uncomfortable for you and me."

"I really don't date, Alan, and I'm not usually the type men come on to."

"What do you mean? Why wouldn't they?"

She thought about those dateless nights she'd endured and released a ragged sigh. "You don't know me very well."

"I don't, but I'd like to." His hand rested on her arm. "If you don't mind."

She felt heat rising to her face. "I don't mind. I'd like to get to know you, too." His hand slipped from her arm, and a smile lit his face.

"Now that we have that cleared up," Juli said, "I'd better get moving before Bill tosses me out on my ear for holding you up."

Alan eyed his workstation. "I'll see you later."

He walked to a glove box, grabbed a pair, then strode to the salad station while Juli wished she could forget her macaroni job and chop lettuce instead.

When the pasta had simmered long enough, Juli drained it and poured the contents into the cheesy sauce. In moments voices drifted from the dining room, and she saw Alan carry one of the large salad bowls to the serving area. She grasped a chafing pan and followed.

As she came through the door, Alan was standing with Angie, preparing to serve the entrée. With her heart sinking, she set the pasta container in front of them then stood behind the salad bowl. She'd gotten her wish to serve the salad, but not the way she'd planned. She clasped the serving spoons and prepared to add the salad mixture to the diners' plates.

The line began, and she sent out smiles and greetings, noting those who seemed to be most heavily burdened. Talking with them was her favorite part of the job, and lately she'd begun thinking about that. During high school she knew she wanted to help people in some way, but now social work had settled in her heart, and she sensed God had put it there. She should have insisted on getting a college degree instead of going right into the family business, but she'd felt she should follow God's commandment to honor her father, who asked her to work in the store and give her mother a rest.

She drew her focus back to the dining hall. Tonight seemed quieter with fewer people in attendance, and she figured they must have found their meals somewhere else. No matter; Juli always thanked God that they fed everyone who came through the door. They never ran out of food. Just like the Lord's unending blessings, she thought.

While Alan chatted with Angie, Juli dragged her flagging spirit from behind the serving counter and headed into the table area as she always did. She moved along the rows of chairs, speaking to people, until an elderly woman called to her as she neared.

She'd never noticed the woman before. She stopped and slipped into an empty chair. "How are you tonight?"

The woman shook her head, her weathered hands clutching the paper napkin. "I miss my home."

Juli wrapped her hand around the woman's, brushing her

wrinkled skin. "What happened?"

"The apartment building was torn down. They called it urban renewal." Tears rimmed the woman's eyes. "I'm too old to work. I have nothing."

Sorrow knotted in Juli's chest. "No family to help you? Children?"

"One's dead, and one can't help—she's struggling herself. Living with a friend."

Juli's throat ached, trying to contain her emotion.

The woman brushed a tear from her eye. "I've seen you talking to the others. You always seem to make people smile."

Her words touched Juli, but today she had no practical answer to solve the woman's problem. She did, however, have a deeper message for the weary woman. "I wish I could help you find a place to stay, but I'll pray about it for you. I hope you know you do have a home for eternity if you love the Lord."

The woman's gaze lifted toward Juli. "That's what keeps me going. I often think of Job. He had real troubles."

Real troubles, yes, but this woman's were huge, too. Awareness struck her. Her own concern about garlic and Gilroy had no effect on anything important. The woman's reflection had given Juli far more direction than she could offer the homeless woman.

"Job said the Lord gives and the Lord takes away," the woman said. "Job was so right, but he ends that verse with even more powerful words. 'May the name of the Lord be praised.' So that's what I do."

Juli squeezed her hand. "You're a true believer, and God loves you."

The woman managed a weak smile and pressed her other frail hand on Juli's. "You're a kind woman. I see why so many like you. Take care of yourself, and thank you for listening to an old lady's mumbling."

"You're not mumbling, and you're very welcome." A smile

filled Juli's heart. She was amazed that this woman with so much against her still had concern for others.

The woman kept Juli's hand pressed between hers. "My name's Rosie."

"Nice to meet you, Rosie. I'm Juli."

When she looked up, Alan stood nearby, listening. She gave the woman another pat and rose, her legs tingling from crouching too long. She moved in Alan's direction, wondering why he'd been eavesdropping.

Alan met her halfway. "I should apologize for listening, but I'm curious how you reach these people. Whatever you say puts smiles on their faces."

"I'm just talking with them." She nodded to one of the regulars seated a table over. "I'll come with you if you're uncomfortable."

He looked at the man then back at Juli. "Is this a challenge?"

She tilted her head in a playful pose. "You can call it anything you want."

He chuckled and moved ahead while she stood back and watched.

As he neared, Alan's face charged with concern when he heard the man's ragged cough. "That sounds bad, sir."

The scruffy man looked up in surprise. "Sir?" He appeared to question the title. He pressed his hand against his chest. "You talkin' to me?"

"I am. Are you taking anything for that cough?"

The man pulled out a grayish, soiled handkerchief and blew his nose. "Don't have nothin' to take, but I'll be fine."

"You'll be fine if you get some care. Do you have a place to sleep tonight?"

His shoulder twitched. "I do all right."

Juli knew he probably slept on the street somewhere, but Alan seemed to know it, too. He gave her a doubtful look. She wanted to step in and offer help, but she couldn't do that to Alan on his first try.

Alan squatted beside the man. "Maybe we can find a place for you tonight." He gave Juli a questioning look.

She beckoned him toward her and kept her voice low. "I called awhile ago for a woman, but they had no room for her. I can try again. They might have a spot in the men's section."

Alan's face lit with hope, and he nodded.

"I'll see what I can do." She squeezed his shoulder and stepped away. Her spirit lifted when the director gave the go-ahead. "But this is it," he said. "That's our last spot."

Forming a telephone with her hand, Juli gave a nod as she returned to Alan with the good news.

"Great," he said, rising from his haunches as he spoke to the man. "My friend here called, and they're holding a bed for you right down the street. Tell them the soup kitchen sent you, and they'll know who you are."

"Thank you," he said, extending a grubby hand to Alan.

Alan shook the man's hand without hesitation.

His loving response to the man touched Juli. She moved away, admiring Alan from the distance.

When the ailing man rose, Alan walked him to the door, pointing down the block, and then turned, his gaze searching the room until he spotted her. He strode to her beside the serving counter. "Looks like everything's pretty well cleaned up tonight." He motioned to the cleared tables.

"A smaller crowd makes it easier," she said, leading the way into the kitchen. She removed her apron, grabbed her handbag from the storage area, and slid it on her shoulder. "I'm glad you came back."

"Me, too."

He seemed to search her face. She didn't know what to say, and then it struck her. "You did a nice job, by the way. He really needed your help."

"He has a bronchial cough. It could lead to pneumonia, or he could have walking pneumonia. His coloring is bad."

Juli deliberated if she should tease him for giving out

medical advice. She decided against it, not wanting to discourage him. Alan was a great addition to the volunteers. She hoped he would invite her for coffee tonight. He fell into step with her, but Juli sensed someone following behind them. She turned and saw Angie looking at Alan.

"Are you leaving?"

Juli frowned, waiting to learn if Alan had made plans with her.

A confused expression flew onto Alan's face. "Leaving? Yes."

Juli sensed Alan wasn't comfortable with Angie's attention, or was it her own wishful thinking?

Angie glanced at Juli then back to Alan. "I wanted to—"

While she hesitated, Juli's heart dipped into a dark hole before popping out again. She grasped her courage, knowing now might be her only chance. "I'll take you up on that coffee invitation, Alan."

Alan's confusion shifted to a smile. "Great."

Juli couldn't believe she'd had the nerve to ask him out for coffee.

Alan turned to the other woman. "Could we talk next week?"

"Next week? Okay." Her look sailed toward Juli like a poison dart before she turned to leave.

"Ready?" Alan asked.

Juli released a pent-up breath. "I sure am."

"Good night," she said to the young woman as she felt Alan's hand clasp her arm.

Juli wanted to sink through the floor. She'd never in her life asked a man to go anywhere, and now that she had, she felt great empathy for Alan because she'd refused his invitation last week. What would she have done if tonight he'd said no?

three

Juli slid into the booth at the diner. Though not in the best area of town, the place appeared clean, and the food smelled good. Her stomach gave a soft growl, and she pressed her hand against it to hold back another grumble.

Alan scooted into the booth, shifted the menu toward her, and leaned back. "Thanks for saving me."

"Saving you?" She probed her memory. "You mean making the phone call? No problem. We do that once in a while when the person is bad off."

His expression melted to a smile. "Thanks for that, too. I meant Angie."

"Angie?" Heat crept up her neck. "Oh."

He looked disconcerted and played with the paper napkin. "She's nice, but I could sense she wanted my attention, and I wasn't interested."

Juli flinched, thinking maybe her invitation had sounded too eager. "I thought you looked uncomfortable."

"To be honest, I really wanted to ask you to stop for coffee. I hesitated because I was afraid I'd come on too strong last week."

"Too strong," she repeated, almost cutting off his sentence. "No. I was really tired." She wanted to tell him how sorry she was that she'd said no. "I hope my invitation didn't seem as desperate as Angie."

"Not at all. I'm glad you said something." He eyed his watch. "Would you like anything besides coffee? I don't want to keep you since you have a long ride, but I'm hungry."

"Thanks. I would," she said, feeling her shoulders relax and reaching for the menu.

They studied the selections and placed their orders, but

when the waitress walked away, Juli felt tongue-tied again.

Alan leaned closer. "May I ask you a question?"

A serious look had settled on his face, and she nodded.

"This is really personal."

Really personal. She looked in his eyes and saw curiosity. "Sure."

"You said you don't date, and I. . .I can't believe your phone isn't ringing off the hook." He looked down at the table. "Is that a religious belief?"

She couldn't control the amazement that sputtered into a chuckle. "Religious? No. Do you think I'm a nun or something?"

He shrugged. "I've never known any woman as attractive as you are who doesn't date."

She drew back and took a lengthy breath. "It's a long story, Alan. I was tall and skinny. I was raised rather strictly, and I've never been one to wear tight clothes or a lot of makeup. I never appealed to most high school boys, and now. . ." Now what? ". . .I have this awful hooked nose that—"

"Hooked nose." He shook his head. "You have a beautiful nose. It's classic. Like a Roman goddess."

"Me? I think you'd better have your eyes checked."

He reached across the table and brushed her cheek. "Maybe you should. Take a long, good look in the mirror sometime. You might have been a gangly teenager once, but today you're really a lovely woman, Juli." His eyes widened. "And don't get me wrong. This isn't a come-on. I think of us as new friends. I'm just being honest."

She felt heat rising to her cheeks again and lowered her gaze to the table. "Thank you."

"You're welcome."

The silence grew again while Juli pondered what Alan had said. Lovely? Roman goddess? The words were alien to her.

"How long have you been a Christian?" Alan's question broke the silence.

Relieved, air whooshed from Juli's lungs. She had wanted to ask him the same question but wasn't sure she wanted to hear his answer. "My folks are Christians, and I grew up knowing Jesus. It was natural, but as an adult I've studied the Word and am convinced Jesus is the Way."

"I thought you were a believer."

She studied his face. From his response she felt afraid to ask. She gave him a moment to say something, and when he didn't, she drew in a lengthy breath. "What about you?"

"Am I a Christian?"

She nodded.

"Absolutely." He grinned. "I figured you knew."

She'd hoped with all her heart. "Next Wednesday there's a special service and speaker at Lighthouse Church a block down from the soup kitchen. Sometimes we go there. Would you like to go? They provide the meals on Tuesday nights."

"To which? The Tuesday soup kitchen or worship?"

She looked at his face and realized he was teasing. She waved away his question. "I supposed that was a little ambiguous. I meant worship." She gave him a playful look.

"Just teasing, but I'd love to if it's not too late when we finish. I need my beauty sleep."

His voice sounded good-natured but tentative. Still, she readily accepted his willingness to go.

In a few minutes her soup and his burger arrived. They were quiet as they bowed their heads and said their own blessings. When Juli took her first bite, she realized how hungry she'd been. The soup tasted homemade and delicious, and Alan looked contented with his burger.

He lifted his head and sniffed. "They're cooking with garlic."

Her chest tightened. "Is that bad?"

"I avoid eating too much of it. It makes me a little nauseated. I probably have an allergy. It's nothing serious."

She winced. "That's too bad. Have you had allergy tests?"

"No. It's never been a serious problem. I just avoid food with garlic."

Juli managed to give him an accepting look, but inside she wanted to scream. She'd finally met someone she felt drawn to, someone she really admired, and now he had a repulsion to garlic. She earned her living knee deep in garlic.

Silence fell between them as they ate. Her thoughts sifted through what she'd just heard.

"Why so quiet?" he asked, breaking the hush.

"My mother taught me not to talk while I eat."

He chuckled. "So true, but I don't always follow my mom's advice."

She grinned and motioned to the bowl. "Besides, I love potato and corn chowder. This is really good."

He'd already finished his burger. He wiped his mouth with the paper napkin and pushed away the empty plate. "How about some pie?"

"I couldn't eat a whole piece, but thanks."

He pulled the small dessert menu from behind the napkin holder. "Let's share."

She agreed, and they chose a pie from the menu. Then Alan flagged the waitress and ordered. When the woman left, he rested his elbow on the table. "Tell me about yourself. I'd love to know everything."

Her pulse skipped while she tried to sort through her life story. "I live up Highway 101 with my parents." She saw a flicker on his face. "I suppose that seems odd for a woman to still live at home, but they have in-law quarters separate from the house, like a guest room, I suppose, and it's convenient. It's close to work."

"What do you do for a living?"

Her muscles tensed. "I work in my dad's store."

"Your father owns a business." He gave an agreeable nod. "What kind of store?"

Juli swallowed. "Produce."

He chuckled. "What else in this 'salad bowl' community?"

"For sure. We're surrounded by every kind of produce farm—lettuce, celery, cauliflower, broccoli, spinach, and even avocados."

He scrunched up his nose. "And don't forget garlic."

She hoped to lead him away from the present course of conversation. "What about you? What do you do?"

"I work at the Community Hospital of the Monterey Peninsula."

"Doing what?"

"Nursing people back to health."

Nursing. "That's a worthy career."

"Worthy but difficult sometimes."

"I heard about the pileup on Highway 1 this morning."

"It was bad. We were running all day. I'm exhausted." He faltered as if he had second thoughts. "But talking with you keeps me awake." His eyes sparkled, and he reached across the table and rested his hand on hers. "You're the sunshine in my day."

"Change a couple of words and you could sing it." While he grinned, she could feel her face growing warm. She hated blushing like a schoolgirl and tried to get a grip on her emotions. "Thanks for the compliment."

He looked more deeply into her eyes. "I would have taken you for a nurse or a social worker. You're so good with the people at the soup kitchen. You surprised me when you said you work in your father's store."

Social worker. His perception validated her thought of a career change.

"I'm sorry. I wasn't putting down your work, but the way you treat those people is a gift."

Juli realized her expression said too much. "I didn't know what I wanted to do before I decided to stick with the family business. My dad needed me in the store." Her dad's deciding she would stay with the family business wasn't the full story, but she didn't want to get into that with Alan. "It gave my mom a break, but now the store is doing well. We have a number of employees, so I manage the business."

"So you're the manager."

She nodded. "But when I was younger, I always loved helping people. I volunteered to visit the elderly homebound in my church when I was a teen, and it was like having all kinds of grandparents. If anything, I'd thought about being in a career that helped people."

"Is your degree in business administration, then?"

Her degree? "My brother majored in business administration."

He looked at her as if waiting for more information.

"I didn't go to college."

"You didn't?"

The look on his face caused a knot in her stomach. "I know you must have attended college, but my job didn't require it. My mom trained me to manage the store."

"Not everyone needs a college education."

She heard an apology in his voice. "I didn't take offense at what you said." She waited for him to continue, but he didn't. "Where did you go to school?

"University of California in San Francisco."

A twinge of regret settled in her chest. He'd gone to one of the best schools possible. She wanted to show she was impressed without sounding envious. "That's a great school."

Alan only nodded.

He seemed so closemouthed about his work, and her stomach knotted when she suspected he felt sorry for her. She wanted him to know it was okay that she didn't have a degree. She didn't want his pity.

"What department do you work in?" She managed to send him a lighthearted grin.

"I work in the ER." He looked uncomfortable.

Juli faltered, realizing the more she probed about his career, the more he would probe about hers. She didn't want to lie, but right now she wasn't ready to tell him about her situation. She might never be ready.

A questioning look grew on Alan's face. "I love my work, but keep in mind, Juli, that it's never too late to start a new career. You'd be a wonderful counselor or social worker. You have the heart for it."

"Thanks." She read sincerity in his eyes. "It's hard to find the time, though."

"God gives each of us talent, but it's in His time, not ours. I love that verse in Ecclesiastes—I think that's it, anyway. 'He has made everything beautiful in its time.' We do things on the Lord's schedule and not our own."

"A long time ago I gave up thoughts of changing my career. At twenty-five I'd find it too hard to go back to school."

He placed his hand on hers again. "Not if it's God's will."

She loved the feeling of his hand on hers, and she felt ashamed she'd given the Lord so little credit. "You're right. To tell you the truth, I don't have a lot of patience."

"Sure you do. Don't give up on your dreams. Maybe someday what you long for will come true."

Looking into his eyes, she realized it could.

રેત

Juli heard a noise outside and opened the door. She waved to her friend Megan as she climbed the staircase to her apartment. "It's been too long," she said, opening her arms.

Megan hurried into her embrace, and Juli gave her a firm hug then motioned her inside.

"I'm so glad you called. I've been thinking of you." Juli headed across the room and halted at the kitchen door, waiting to offer her friend a soda.

Megan plopped onto the love seat. "I hope they were good thoughts."

"Naturally. Someone at the soup kitchen asked me when I started working there, and I told him about your inviting me and then pooping out."

Megan sat straighter, her eyes glinting. "Did you say *him?*"

Juli held up her hand like a traffic cop. "A guy I helped train on his first night."

"Hmm. Sounds interesting."

Juli propped her hand on her hip. "Don't start anything. I just met him."

Megan grinned. "But there's always hope."

"Only in your mind." She shook her finger at her as if Megan were a naughty schoolgirl then motioned toward the kitchen, wanting to change the subject. She liked Alan, but hoping too hard could only bring a letdown. "How about a soda?"

"That's good for me."

Juli stepped into her kitchen and pulled two drinks from the refrigerator. She emptied chips into a bowl and carried them and the sodas into the living room. After setting the bowl and a drink in front of Megan, Juli settled into an easy chair.

The conversation drifted to mutual friends, work, and high school memories. When the conversation centered on school, Juli recalled Melanie's visit. "Guess who came into the store a couple of weeks ago."

"George Clooney."

She waved her comment away. "Don't I wish? No. Someone we knew in high school."

Megan searched her face. "Don't tell me. Melanie Ives."

"How did you guess?"

"The look on your face." Megan twisted her face into a silly expression.

Juli couldn't help but chuckle. "I know it's been seven years, and I should be over it, but Melanie had to mention the bouquet." She made pretentious motions with her hands, mimicking Melanie. "And she did it in front her sorority sister who was slumming at the garlic market." Her uncontrolled envy startled her, and she asked God's forgiveness.

"Juli. It's not like you to sound so catty."

"I know. It just got under my skin. I'm sorry."

Megan waved away the topic. "Let's talk about something interesting." She scooted forward on the sofa. "Tell me about him."

"Him?"

"Don't be coy. This guy you met at the soup kitchen."

Juli's nerves pinged with Megan's questions, and she knew Megan wouldn't give up. On edge, Juli reached for her soda, bumped her hand against it, and caught it before it fell from the table. "I don't know the man that well. He's nice, and I trained him. That's it."

"Sounds interesting. Maybe I'll show up next week so I can see this guy. Do you still go on Wednesday?"

"Wednesday. Right." Juli's heart sank. Megan was so pretty with her long blond hair and blue eyes.

Megan wriggled back against the sofa. "I'll have to see if I can make it. I should have continued volunteering. It's good to do things for others."

"I agree." But not now. Megan was so attractive. Concern prickled up Juli's back. Did Alan mean something to her? Juli had insinuated the opposite; yet saying aloud that she cared about him might raise her hopes too high. She decided to let well enough alone and hope Megan would forget by next Wednesday.

№

"Wait up!"

Alan looked over his shoulder and stopped as Tom caught up with him.

"Where're you headed?"

The question left Alan no choice but to tell the truth. "The soup kitchen." He felt his brow wrinkle. "You're not really interested in going, are you?"

Tom shrugged. "How long are you there?"

"That's hard to say. A big crowd takes more time to feed.

Last week we were finished by eight thirty or maybe nine."

Digging his hands into his pockets, Tom appeared to ponder the information. "Can I go for an hour or so? You know, just to check it out."

The comment irked Alan. He guessed what really interested Tom. "An hour's work is better than nothing," he said, admitting he had to think of the needy people and not his own concern about Tom.

Tom nodded. "I'll follow you."

Alan motioned toward the staff parking. "I'll wait for you by the exit." He hurried ahead, hoping Juli wouldn't be beguiled by Tom's flirtatiousness.

He grumbled to himself as he waited by the exit gate. When he saw Tom's car behind him, he inserted his identification card and waited as the exit arm lifted; then he rolled onto the side street. Tom pulled from the exit and followed Alan as he continued to Highway 1, driving slow enough for Tom to stay in his view. Once in Seaside, Alan guided him to a parking spot behind the soup kitchen.

Inside, the scent of hot dogs struck him when they came through the door. Bill greeted them and after the introduction led Tom away for training. Angie nabbed Alan before he could check his station.

She gave him a smile. "Remember me?"

"I do," Alan said, trying to slip away to follow Bill and Tom.

She caught his arm. "I could use some help opening these cans."

Alan eyed the large containers of fruit cocktail and gave a huff. He hoped Angie hadn't heard it; he forced himself to remember he had volunteered to do charity work and not chase Juli.

"I'd better check my station, Angie."

"You're here. I already checked."

"Are you sure?"

She nodded.

He drew up his shoulders and grasped one of the large cans, trying to halt his exasperation. While he detached the lids, Angie dished the fruit into bowls, and Alan realized it could be a long project. With Angie's concentration on filling the dishes, Alan glanced over his shoulder and spotted Tom. This time he didn't care who heard his huff. Bill had asked Juli to show Tom around, and Alan saw the satisfied expression on his coworker's face.

An idea formed. He'd make sure to work in the food line beside Juli. At least they could talk without Tom hanging around. Feeling better about the situation, Alan cranked the can opener and finished the job in record time.

"There you go," he said, sliding the last can closer to her. Before she could ask him to help dish up the fruit, he made his way across the room to Juli and Tom. "I can help with the lettuce," he said, grabbing a head. But before he could wield the knife, Bill came past.

"They need help over there," Bill said, shifting Alan's attention to another area. "That's your station."

"My station?" Alan looked at Angie, realizing she'd tricked him. When he tried to catch Juli's attention, she was laughing at something Tom had apparently told her. Alan normally loved her laugh, but not when it was with Tom.

Disappointed in his overzealous feelings for a woman he barely knew, Alan turned away and strode to the butcher-block table.

"Here you go," the worker said, sliding him a knife and tapping his blade on a bag of onions. "Everyone likes these with hot dogs."

Onions. Alan's stomach knotted. Juli and Tom were tearing lettuce into small pieces, and he had to chop onions. He pulled out a large one, removed the skin, and attacked it with vengeance.

"Careful," the man said. "You'll be bleeding all over the butcher block."

Feeling as if he'd been sliced and diced beneath the man's questioning gaze, Alan shrank in humiliation and mumbled that he'd be more careful.

The juice from the onion smarted his eyes, and tears welled on his lower lashes then rolled down his cheeks. He brushed them away with his arm and noticed Juli watching him. She sent him a hello wave by wiggling her fingers, and he tried to grin back and forget the onions.

When voices sounded from the dining room, the workers headed to the serving area. As Alan scraped the last of the diced onions from the butcher block, he felt a hand on his arm.

"They gave you the rotten job."

Juli's voice glided to his ears, and he looked into her blurred face.

She lifted her fingers and brushed the tears from his cheeks. "It wasn't that bad, was it?"

A grin settled on his mouth. "No. I loved every minute of it."

She laughed, and this time he loved the sound because she was with him.

"We'd better get out there," he said, grasping the onion container.

She walked beside him to the doorway, her arm brushing against his, and to his delight Bill flagged him to the hot dog station and Juli to the buns. Together finally, he thought, even though it was the hottest job on a warm day. When he looked around, he found that Tom had vanished.

While Juli stood beside him with the open bun, he slipped the hot dog inside and listened to her friendly conversation with the homeless. He looked into the crowd, seeing a few bow their heads. But most eagerly ate the food that had to last many of them twenty-four hours or more.

Pushing aside his grumbling, Alan felt blessed. His own stomach was full, and the nicest woman in the room stood beside him. When he noticed Juli motioning, he looked down and saw an empty bun and a woman and young boy waiting on the other side of the counter. *There but for the grace of God go I.* The sentence filled his head, words that had such strong meaning for him.

Sorry he'd held up the line with his musing, Alan dropped a hot dog into the roll and gave Juli a wink. "Give the young man an extra one. He's a growing boy."

He remembered someone had done that for him once so long ago.

four

Juli beckoned to Alan. "We'll be late if we don't get moving," she called.

He lifted the bucket into the air. "What about cleaning up?"

She loved the way he'd come on the scene and seemed to give the job his all, from onions to the cleanup detail. He never complained. "Bill lets people go early to make the service on time. Others are willing to clean up."

He held up one finger and pointed to the storage room then came bounding toward her and linked his arm in hers. "Let's go."

He pulled her toward the front door, but she stopped him. "Everyone's waiting in the back."

His smile faded. "Everyone?"

She realized he hadn't understood her invitation. "I mentioned sometimes others like to go along. I thought you knew."

Alan's mouth tugged into a half smile, and Juli sensed he'd struggled to put it there.

"I guess I didn't hear that part. It's not a problem." He released her arm and strode toward the back door of the kitchen.

But it was a problem, and she knew it. What could she do? Others liked to attend the service, and she'd always been happy they wanted to hear God's Word. Thoughts tossed in her head as Juli decided not to say anything more. She hoped Alan would understand and enjoy the praise service with the rest of them.

The others joined them as they came outside, and they headed down the alley to the sidewalk then made their way to the church. Music streamed through the open door, and as they stepped inside, the spirit of the worship filled her. Among those who had come were some of the homeless who found strength in the Lord.

The group slid into chairs, most sitting together. Before she could slip in beside Alan, a new volunteer she hadn't met had shifted between them, and she had no way to correct the situation without making the newcomer feel unwelcome. She leaned around the man and smiled, but Alan didn't smile back. Instead he shrugged and looked toward the platform.

Juli managed to keep her eyes forward and ignore him. When she'd invited him to attend worship, she'd never said it was a date. She would have liked that, but a number of people attended the special services together, and it had become a tradition. They gathered by the back door and walked over together.

With Alan's silence, Juli's thoughts drifted. She recalled Megan had said she'd be at the soup kitchen tonight, but she hadn't shown up. The music began, and voices lifted in praise, but tonight her voice seemed constricted. She gave in and glanced Alan's way, but he only looked toward the praise group singing.

Juli lowered her head. Her purpose here was to worship and not stare at Alan. She felt ashamed of her preoccupation and sent up a prayer asking for God's help, but as she prayed, an uncomfortable weight pressed against her stomach. The heat of the room and the stench of those who didn't have the luxury of a shower filled her nostrils then churned inside her. Unable to sit any longer, she explained to the person sitting beside her that she had to leave. She looked at Alan then decided to let it go.

While the crowd stood, clapping their hands to the rhythm of the music, Juli slid past the worshipers to the end of the row and hurried outside. She drew in a deep breath of warm fresh air and wondered why she felt so ill. She looked down the dimly lit street toward the soup kitchen then lifted her shoulders and strode toward her car. She would explain everything to Alan the next time she saw him.

Each dark doorway sent a trickle of fear along her limbs. Anyone could be hidden against the inset of the shop doors, the homeless or someone out for no good. Juli had always walked back from worship to her car with the others, and she hadn't thought about being in a crime area. She moved closer to the street and increased her pace.

The farther Juli walked away from the church, the more edgy she became. She gripped her shoulder bag to her side and increased her speed. As she approached the corner with one more block to go, a hand jutted out from a shadowy store entrance. A sharp pressure jammed against her shoulder as the strap of her purse dug into her skin. Fear clenched her throat. She tried to pull away but suddenly tripped over something— was it the thief's leg?—and fell to the ground. Her handbag was yanked from her arm, and she heard heavy steps running off.

"Stop!" An angry voice cut through the night.

She heard footsteps again, this time coming closer, then Alan's breathless words. "Are you okay?"

"Yes, but he grabbed my bag."

Alan dashed off in pursuit of the purse snatcher.

Tears rolled from her eyes, and nausea rose to her throat. She swallowed the acrid bile and sat a moment to gain control while her mind went over all the things she'd have to replace. A new driver's license, her cell phone, her house key, credit cards—so many things she'd have to cancel and—

She pushed herself upward, her hands stinging from skidding across the concrete sidewalk. Brushing away the dirt, she felt the burning sensation increase; she saw the skin peeled back but no serious damage. She looked up and noticed a police car heading her way. It rolled to a stop at the curb, and the officer leaned out of the window.

"Are you okay, miss?"

She nodded. "I'm fine. Just frightened." To her surprise,

Alan stepped from the other side of the vehicle. Knowing he was there helped her feel more secure.

"Can you give me a description?" The officer had left his car and was standing beside her.

"I didn't see him. He jumped out of there." She pointed to the shadowy door entrance.

"That's always the way. Come down to the station if you want to make a report."

"I'm fine. Thanks."

He got back into his car, nodded to her, and drove off.

Alan drew closer. "Are you sure the guy didn't hurt you?" He put his arm around her.

Tears blurred her eyes, and she released the torrent.

Alan nestled her against his shoulder.

"I'm sorry," she whispered when she'd gained control. "I didn't mean to cry."

He stepped back. "You're sorry? Juli, you could have been injured or killed. Thugs will do anything for money."

"I was so stupid to leave the church, but—"

He pressed his finger to her lips. "But nothing." He lifted her hands and saw her skinned palms. "You need to get some antiseptic on these hands."

"I'm fine. . .except for my shoulder bag."

His expression changed to a silly grin. "Here."

He was clasping her bag in his other hand.

Her eyes opened wide. "Wow! I guess you're my superhero. How did you get it?"

"When the kid darted around the corner, the cop pulled up, and he dropped your purse and ran. The officer made a call then drove me back here."

Grateful, she smiled and patted his arm. "You saved me from having to replace everything in it."

"You can thank the cop. He saw me chasing the guy and figured out what had happened. I'm sure that's what scared the guy away."

"Praise God for that." She hugged her bag to her chest. "How can I thank you?"

"Now that's an interesting question." He linked his arm with hers and took a step toward the car then stopped. "But first tell me why you left the church."

She lowered her head, realizing the scare had replaced her sick feeling. Juli told him about the heat and her nausea. "I wasn't thinking about the walk back to the car."

"No more of that. Never walk alone. Promise me."

Her pulse skipped at the concern in his voice. "I promise. It was thoughtless."

"That's right. It was."

His grin unsettled her. "Don't be so enthusiastic."

"The only thing I'm enthusiastic about is taking you up on that offer."

She faltered and turned to him. "What offer?"

"You asked what you can do to thank me."

In the dim light she could still see the twinkle in his eye. "And what would that be?"

"Seeing me sometime outside the soup kitchen."

"I'm seeing you right now."

"Seeing as in a date."

"You want me to go out on a date with you?" Her heart thundered.

"It would make me very happy. Plus it would pay off your indebtedness."

"I'm known for always paying my bills."

He slipped his arm around her shoulder and gave her a quick hug. "That's what I hoped."

Her laugh joined his. Somehow Alan usually managed to say the right thing, and tonight it was the most right thing she'd heard in a long time.

❧

Alan ripped off his protective gloves, moved to the next patient, pulled on a fresh pair of gloves, and stepped beside the nurse. He eyed the monitors then studied the deep gash in the patient's chest. "Maintain compression." The wound lay too close to the heart for his expertise. "Call surgical. Stat."

Another major car pileup. His mind spun with the horror one speeding driver could cause. He tore off his gloves and tossed them in the receptacle then brushed the perspiration from his eyes and glanced at the clock. His heart sank. His date with Juli.

As the patient with the chest wound was being wheeled to surgery, Alan drew in a lengthy breath, thinking of the stressful day. The man had been the last injury brought in from the accident, and Alan knew he could leave.

He took the hall toward the locker room then veered away and strode to the cafeteria. He'd been without food for hours.

Why had he been so negligent? Juli had suggested meeting him in Monterey. She insisted, and he hadn't even asked for her telephone number. Hours had passed since they were to meet. He could picture her waiting fifteen minutes, a half hour, an hour, then leaving. She'd be long gone and angrier than a cornered bear, and he wouldn't blame her.

Alan headed for the sandwich bar, selected a tuna-filled pita wrap, and paid for it and a coffee at the cashier. He spotted a table looking into the courtyard and sank into a chair. Though he was hungry, his appetite had waned at the realization he'd missed his first date with Juli. What would she think of him? If she heard about the accident, she may have guessed. If not, he was history.

A hand pressed against his shoulder, and he jumped.

"What's up with you?" Tom pulled out a chair and sat down.

"Another accident today."

"I know. We had a full house in the surgical unit."

Tom eyed him, and Alan waited for his next question.

"What's really troubling you? You've handled a truckload of accident cases. That's nothing new."

Alan sank deeper into the chair, not wanting to tell Tom, whose mouth was often bigger than the Pacific. "I had a date tonight."

Tom shrugged. "She'll understand. Getting involved with a physician makes it part of the deal."

Guilt rolled up Alan's back. "She doesn't know I'm a physician."

"You're kidding." His eyes widened like two blue moons.

Alan shook his head. "I have my reasons."

"Who is she? She can't be from here."

Alan gave up. "Juli. From the soup kitchen. But listen— I want you to keep your mouth shut if you're going back there." He gave Tom a probing look. "When you were there last time, you didn't make the big announcement I was a physician, did you?"

"I didn't say anything about you. Why would I? I figured they knew, and I talked about me."

"They don't know, and I want to keep it that way. It's not why I'm there, and it's important to me that it's not broadcast around."

A crooked grin grew on Tom's face. "So the good Christian boy has told a lie."

"No, I haven't."

Tom's smile slid to a questioning look. "How did you avoid that?"

"Juli asked what I did, and I said I worked at the hospital in the ER and nursed people back to health. That's all the truth."

"She thinks you're a nurse, then, I suppose. Why the secret? You should be proud you're a physician, pal."

How could he answer this question without going into his background and his motivation? "I don't have to be a physician to volunteer at the soup kitchen. I want to be me and not a doctor. Can you understand?"

Tom frowned. "I guess not."

Alan didn't understand himself either, but it was important

to him. "Can you keep your mouth shut? Please don't say anything to anyone. Let me do that when I'm ready."

Tom shook his head. "Whatever you say, pal."

Alan took a bite of his sandwich, wishing the subject hadn't come up. Maybe he was being foolish about this, but for once in his life he wanted to be Alan Louden, volunteer at a soup kitchen. He didn't want to be anyone special, and he certainly couldn't practice medicine at a soup kitchen.

He lifted his gaze and saw Tom staring at him. "What?"

"I'm trying to figure you out. That's not easy."

"Sorry."

"Then tell me about Juli. I didn't know you had a thing for her, although I don't blame you."

"I don't have a *thing* for her. She's a nice woman, and things fell in place for me to ask her for a date."

"What kind of things?"

Alan gave up again. Tom was worse than a nosy neighbor, so he told him about the purse-snatching incident.

"You're a hero in her eyes." He rose and slapped Alan on the back. "Good thinking."

"I didn't plan it."

Tom squeezed his shoulder. "I know. Maybe it was providence." He waved. "I'm not off duty yet, so I'd better get back."

Alan watched him vanish around the tray return and let his word sink in. *Providence.* To Alan that meant God. Was meeting Juli God's doing? For the first time since he'd left the ER, his shoulders relaxed. If this were God's doing, then he had nothing to worry about.

略

Juli parked her car in the Del Monte Shopping Center outside Elli's Great American Restaurant. She'd agreed to meet Megan for dinner and then shopping, but her heart wasn't in it. The mall was crowded, and she'd stood much of the day at the Garlic Garden pitching in to help with the busy store again and watching her paperwork pile up.

"I can't fool myself," she mumbled, sliding from her car and heading for the restaurant. She knew her non-date with Alan had set her on edge. She hadn't expected him to stand her up. He seemed too real and thoughtful. It took her back to high school days when she'd longed for a date, and then when one finally happened, she'd been stood up. So many disappointments.

Juli reviewed over and over what she and Alan had agreed on. She was to meet him in Monterey Joe's parking lot at six. Alan worked in Monterey, and it saved her from admitting she lived in Gilroy. Another totally useless worry. She had to give that problem to the Lord.

Juli had even hoped she'd set her watch wrong—anything but to be stood up. The time had been accurate. That night she'd waited until after 6:45, every minute torture.

"Hey, girlfriend!"

Juli turned toward Megan's voice and saw her coming through the parking lot, waving.

She waved back and headed for Elli's.

Megan greeted her outside the entrance and flopped her arm over her shoulder. "You look tired. Up late?"

"No," Juli said, wanting to stay away from the subject but knowing that wouldn't be possible.

"No?" Megan opened the door and motioned her inside. "Something's wrong?"

Juli let the hostess distract them as she guided them to a table and handed them each a menu. Juli flipped it open and studied the fare, hoping that time would move their conversation to a new topic. "I think I'll get something fattening like the All-American Burger." She closed the menu. "And their fresh-cut fries."

"Hmm. That's not like you. You're always watching calories." She tossed her menu on the table. "What happened?"

"Nothing." She could say that honestly.

Megan didn't appear to be dissuaded "What *didn't* happen, then?"

"Come on, Megan. If I wanted to talk about it, I would." She folded her arms across her chest. "I thought this was a fun evening for us. Shopping and dinner. Grill the burger, not me."

Megan grasped the menu again and flipped it open. She didn't say a word, and Juli's chest ached that she'd spoken so harshly to her friend.

Juli waited a moment then spoke. "Megan."

Her friend's eyes remained focused on the menu.

"Listen. I'm sorry. Please forgive me."

Megan didn't move for a second; then her head inched upward over the menu, and she looked into Juli's eyes. "I didn't mean to grill you. I'm your friend, and I care what happens to you."

"I know you do." A waitress stopped at their table, and Juli faltered. "Let's order, and then I'll tell you."

When the waitress had gone, Juli told her about Alan and the purse snatcher.

"Why did you go out on that street alone at night? You know better than that."

"I wasn't thinking."

"Juli, you treat the homeless with such compassion, but not everyone out there in the world is as kind as you are. You have to be careful."

"I know. I wasn't feeling well, and—" She thought back to that night. "I'd upset Alan unintentionally, and I think that just got to me."

"Upset him?"

She explained the misunderstanding then continued. "But I felt better when he ran after the guy who took my bag. He brought it back, and the whole situation led to a date. I'm so startled he stood me up."

"He stood you up? Didn't he at least call to explain what happened?"

The question sank into her thoughts like an anchor. "I never gave him my phone number. He never asked, and I didn't think about it. Not too bright of me."

"Or him," Megan said.

The waitress appeared with their drinks, and the conversation halted until she left.

Juli grasped the iced tea and took a long, cool drink.

Megan moved her glass to the side of her plate. "You said Alan works at the hospital in the ER. Did you know about the horrible pileup yesterday? He might have gotten held up at work."

"What accident? You mean the one on Highway 1?"

"No, that was a week or so ago. This was a different one. A speeder lost control, and a number of cars were involved. I think it was on Highway 68."

The possibility washed over her. Had Alan been held up at work? An accident should have entered her mind. She'd seen enough ER TV shows with all the doctors and nurses scurrying around after a highway tragedy. She knew his work would come first.

"You've made an assumption and judged Alan without knowing what really happened."

God's Word flew into her thoughts. *Do not judge, and you will not be judged. Do not condemn, and you will not be condemned. Forgive, and you will be forgiven.* Juli lowered her head. "I'm too inexperienced with these emotions, Megan. It's been too long since I've even given one look at a man, and now I'm so afraid."

"Afraid?"

"Of being hurt, I guess. I really like Alan. He's intelligent and funny, but I see something in his eyes. A kind of compassion or deep hurt. Something. I don't know him well enough yet to understand, but I know it's there."

"Then give the relationship time."

"I suppose I'm rushing things, but it's just a feeling—"

"Maybe it's the Lord talking to you. You need to listen."

Juli's fingers uncoiled from the glass. "I wish this weren't so important to me. I feel like a kid instead of an adult."

Megan slipped her hand over Juli's. "When the heart is involved, we're kids again. Talk to the Lord. Let Him guide your heart, Juli. You just met this guy, but if it's part of the Lord's plan, then don't worry."

A ragged breath escaped. "Thanks, Megan. I needed to hear that." She thought for a moment then moved to a new topic. "I thought you were coming to the soup kitchen last week."

"I meant to, but things happened."

"Alan brought a friend with him."

"Really." Megan grinned. "Are you playing matchmaker?"

"Maybe. I'll see you next week. Right?"

five

Alan wiped perspiration from his palms as he opened the soup kitchen door. He didn't know what to expect from Juli, but he couldn't blame her. Any man who asked a woman for a date and then didn't write down her telephone number was a jerk. He was one with a capital *J*.

He scanned the workers while he moved through the kitchen, and his heart sank. He headed for the doorway to the dining room and glanced inside, hoping, but Juli wasn't there either. He checked the list and moved to his station, another hot job at the oven. Eyeing the recipe on the corn muffin bag, he watched the door with his peripheral vision. He felt his shoulders slump.

Forcing them to rise, he reviewed why he was here. His first purpose was to serve the needy. *There but for the grace of God go I.* He let the words wash over him, remembering the struggles from his youth and thanking the Lord for so many blessings he'd received. A scholarship to college made his life different. His mother couldn't have afforded tuition, and even though he worked, he wouldn't have had enough. Every extra penny went to help his mother.

When Alan looked at the faces of the homeless, he saw his own. He wondered if he'd ever adjust to being in a different financial position now. As a physician, he'd earned so much more than he'd ever dreamed. Though he still helped his family, he had a small condo, and that was more than anyone needed, unless—

A prickle of awareness moved along his neck, and he turned. Juli stood inside the doorway, the shoulder bag he'd recaptured hanging over her arm. Alan stood motionless, not knowing the best approach. Juli shifted, and her gaze met his.

He pressed his hand to his chest and mouthed, "Sorry."

She gave a brief nod, stopped to talk with Bill, then headed his way.

Alan set down the bag of cornmeal mix and walked toward her, a muscle ticking in his jaw. "Juli, I'm so—"

"Was it the pileup?"

Relief flooded him. "Yes, and I didn't have your telephone number. When I got out of there, I tried to look you up, but I didn't find your name in the book, and I had no idea where you lived, except north of Monterey."

"My friend Megan told me about it. I'd hoped that was the reason."

"I felt like a heel. I can't imagine what you thought of me."

Juli's eyes darkened, and he wondered what she was thinking. If the look reflected what she thought of him, he didn't want to know.

"Let's forget it," she said. "I understand."

"But I don't want to forget the date. Can we try again? This Saturday I'm off."

She hesitated.

To reassure her, he added, "I want your telephone number this time."

Finally she grinned. "Same plans as last time?"

Bill's voice cut into their conversation. "Let's get busy. Time's fleeting."

Alan touched her shoulder. "Let's talk about it later."

She nodded and moved away, and he went back to the corn muffin mix. As he worked, his frustration rose. He saw Juli busy near the stove, and with her was the guy from the restaurant. He gave her a playful poke. He didn't like what he saw. Apparently neither did Juli. She gave the guy a look he'd never seen her give before, and from her body language, he suspected Juli had told him to keep his hands to himself. Alan's spirits lifted, and the next time he looked, the guy had moved to another station.

Happy, Alan turned on the huge oven, and with the utensils gathered in front of him, he measured the mix, added the eggs and liquid, then followed the directions and spooned the goop into the muffin pans. Although many of the greatest chefs were men, Alan had somehow missed the talent of getting the mix into the muffin cups. He pulled off a paper towel, wet it, and tried to wipe away the excess.

A snicker sounded behind him, and he saw Juli with a wide grin on her face. "You're no Wolfgang Puck, are you?"

"Isn't he a character in Shakespeare's *Midsummer*—"

This time she laughed. "He's a chef, but you're partly right. Puck is a character in a Shakespeare play. I read it in high school."

He'd read it in college, and once again it irked him that Juli hadn't had a chance to reach her dream. He could picture her trying to help her family as he had done, and he felt proud. Though he never wanted to talk about his past, he and Juli apparently had that in common.

He slid the muffin tins into the oven and started another batch, his eye on the clock. The muffins needed to be ready in a half hour, but the time meant more to him than that. He'd have a chance to talk with her. When the next batch was ready, he pulled the other tins out of the oven to cool.

While transferring the muffins to the serving tray, Alan noticed Juli greeting an attractive blond. The friend she'd mentioned, he guessed, and now Alan wondered if the other woman would stand in their way of talking privately later.

Feeling like a novice at dating, Alan struggled with his emotions. He'd never felt this way about a woman so quickly— at least not in his adult life. His teen years were filled with emotional ups and downs that never settled in one place. His finances held him back from dating anyone except those in his situation, and then a walk on a summer evening or an occasional discount movie had been the highlight of his dating.

Noise rose from the dining room as those waiting outside crowded into the building. He carried the large trays to the serving counter. Juli and her friend were side by side with soup ladles, and the salad bowls stood between him and Juli, so he turned his attention to the line of hungry people, smiled, and served the muffins and butter.

Time seemed to drag, but finally the crowd thinned. Juli had wandered among the crowd as always, this time with her friend at her side. Both women spoke with the needy men and women, but only Juli's face seemed to reflect the sincere concern and compassion that made her so appealing.

Alan helped pull the serving dishes into the kitchen then grasped the bucket filled with disinfectant and water. He picked up a large cloth and headed back into the dining room to perform his usual task. When Juli finally noticed him, he nodded but let her make the first move. Tonight he felt uncomfortable, both with the bungled date and with two sets of eyes looking at him as he worked.

"Alan."

Juli's voice reached him, and he turned.

"This is Megan. She's the one who told me about the accident last Saturday."

"Thanks," he said, reaching out to shake her hand, but he stopped himself and wiped his hand on a towel to dry off the soapy water.

"Nice to meet you, Alan." She gave him a grin. "You owe me one for the save."

It took him a moment to realize she meant his missed date. "I knew I was in hot water."

She chuckled. "Boiling water."

"Hush," Juli said, bumping her hip into Megan's. She reached into her pocket and handed him a piece of paper. "This is for you."

He glanced at the note and slipped it into his pocket. "Thanks." He studied Megan, wondering if she understood their conversation. "Are you leaving?"

Juli nodded. "Megan and I are stopping somewhere to chat."

He tried to keep from showing his disappointment. "Have fun."

Juli took a step backward then halted. "By the way, where's your friend?"

"Tom?"

She nodded.

"He had to get home tonight. The family was celebrating his nephew's birthday. He turned four today, and he loves Tom."

"I just wondered." She motioned toward the note she'd given him. "Call me."

She waved and moved off, leaving Alan to figure out why she'd asked about Tom.

&

Juli relived her telephone call from Alan as she slipped into a new dress she'd picked up at Ross's during her outing with Megan on Saturday. It was a coral and white halter sundress with a sweeping skirt that looked not too casual and not too dressy. She hoped it fit the occasion. She slipped on natural-colored strappy sandals, added a clutch bag, then eyed herself in the mirror. She cringed when she saw her hair curling into frizz, a casualty of the humidity.

Alan insisted he pick her up at home, and she insisted not. Until she knew where things were going, she didn't want her parents' questioning looks. Though she had her own apartment, living so close meant they were able to watch her comings and goings. It made her feel like a child. Alan said he would go along with her request this once and instead suggested they meet by the aquarium on Cannery Row in Monterey. She loved the old part of town that had been brought to life in John Steinbeck's novels.

The traffic moved well until she hit Seaside. Maybe if she

was late, she'd make Alan worry this time. "Sorry, Lord," she said, disliking her "get even" feelings. She'd lived too long wishing she could have gotten even for hurtful things of the past. That wasn't the way of a Christian.

When she turned toward Cannery Row, the traffic bogged even worse, and after finding a parking spot, Juli tried to shake off her stress. She grabbed her clutch bag and sweater, locked her car, and hurried toward the aquarium.

Nearing the building, she spotted Alan leaning against a signpost. He waved when he spotted her. She waved back, feeling as if her feet were flying beneath her.

"No mishaps this time," she said when she reached him.

He studied her a moment before he spoke. "You look amazing. Like a spring garden."

"Thanks." She gazed at his periwinkle-hued polo shirt and noticed it was nearly the color of his eyes. She wanted to tell him he looked amazing, too, but she felt it would be forward.

They stood a moment in anxious silence until he grasped her elbow and pointed. "We're heading that way for dinner." His smile was as warm as the June sun.

She nodded and walked beside him, more comfortable this time in their silence. When Alan stopped, he motioned to a doorway. "I thought we'd try the Blue Moon Bistro. I've never been there, but I've heard good things."

"It looks expensive."

"You're worth it, and it makes up for last week. I still feel bad about that."

"You don't owe me anything, Alan. I really understand. You were needed on your job. You had no choice."

"Thanks."

She sent him a reassuring smile as he led her inside, her steps bouncing with anticipation. Inside the dining room she hesitated, viewing the lovely surroundings. Every table overlooked Monterey Bay with a decor of soft blues and greens that reminded her of the sea.

They were led to a table along the windows and given menus. Her eyes focused first on the view, the late afternoon sun dotting the seafoam green water. Seagulls soared against a deepening blue sky. She pulled her gaze from the view to the menu, and when she opened it, the prices jumped from the page.

"Do you like steak?" Alan's voice cut through her thoughts.

Her attention skipped to the entrées, and she held her breath. "Could we share?"

"Share?" A frown replaced his smile.

"Like the pie. I thought—"

"Do you like steak?"

She nodded.

"Good. Do you mind if I order?"

She shook her head, embarrassed that she'd suggested sharing, but she wanted to save his money. She had no idea how much income a nurse made, but steaks at this price couldn't be everyday fare.

When the waitress appeared, Alan placed their order then turned to her. "What would you like to drink?"

"Water's fine."

"Iced tea?" His eyes studied hers.

She nodded.

The waitress left, and Juli turned again to the sunlight dancing on the ripples of the bay. "It's gorgeous, Alan. Thank you so much."

"You're welcome. I have another surprise when we leave. I hope you don't mind." His lips curved into a smile.

"You like surprises."

He nodded. "Good ones."

"Me, too, but not bad ones. I've had too many of those." She wished she hadn't been so open.

He didn't ask, and the tension in her shoulders subsided. She studied his profile as he looked at the bay. The sun had begun to lower toward the horizon, and she could imagine the magnificent sunset that would follow.

"Tell me about yourself." The words sailed from her mouth without her control.

Alan's smile tightened, and she sensed he didn't like to talk about himself. She could understand that, because she didn't either, so why had she opened the door to sharing personal information?

He shrugged. "Nothing much to tell. Mom lives near Marina. I have four siblings and—"

"Five kids in your family?"

He nodded. "Two brothers, one's deceased, and three sisters. Two live on the East Coast. I'm the youngest. My dad died so long ago I don't remember him."

"I'm sorry. That must have been tough on your mom." She couldn't imagine being without her dad, even though he'd put many demands on her. She knew in her heart that he simply wanted her to follow God's Word.

"It was, but let's not talk about that now." He reached over and rested his hand on hers. "We're here to have a good time."

The waitress arrived and ended the serious moment, and they focused on their dinners, with further conversation only about the delicious food and ambience of the restaurant. The tender steak was excellent, served with a wild mushroom sauce and garlic mashed potatoes. She noticed Alan had replaced his with red potatoes.

"You're quiet," Alan said, setting his iced tea glass on the table.

"Enjoying the food and the view."

"I'm glad." He pushed aside his plate. "We should leave room for dessert. Did you notice the menu? Warm chocolate lava cake. That has to be enticing."

She grinned, thinking it wasn't nearly as enticing as he was. "I couldn't eat a morsel."

"Really. How about tiramisu?"

The look on his face made her laugh. "That's hard to resist, but no. I'm filled to the brim."

"Me, too," he said. "You fill me to the brim."

Feeling a flush, she thanked him and looked again at the golden speckles glinting on the water and thought of how the Lord blessed her every day. Like Alan, He offered surprises beyond measure, and meeting Alan had been one of those wonderful unexpected gifts. *Thank You, Lord,* she thought.

Comfort wrapped around Juli as she sat in quiet conversation with Alan. Nothing profound was said, but he talked again about her compassion with the homeless and how much he enjoyed her company. Bolstered by their open conversation, she admitted she loved being with him. "Did you know your shirt matches the color of your eyes?"

His mouth curved into a smile. "I just slipped it over my head. I'm not even sure what color my eyes are."

"Periwinkle. A beautiful shade of dusky lilac blue, like periwinkle."

"And yours are creamy milk chocolate."

His hand slipped over hers for a moment before he checked his watch. "I hate to leave, but I think we'd better get going."

Juli rose, curious to learn the surprise he'd planned. But while they were heading back on Highway 1, she was surprised in a different way.

"Do you like Tom?" Alan's voice jarred the quiet.

"Tom?" She felt her forehead crinkle with a frown. "I don't really know him."

"You asked about him, and I wondered."

She thought back to that day and remembered Megan had been there. Was Alan jealous? Butterfly wings tripped through her chest. "Tom seemed nice, and I'd told Megan he might be there."

His strained expression softened to a grin. "Ah, so you're matchmaking."

"Not really, but"—the truth struck her—"possibly."

He removed his hand from the steering wheel and brushed her arm. "That's kind of cute. Tom should be there next week.

I'll tell him he was missed."

"Not by me, please."

"Guaranteed. I'll tell him about Megan."

He focused on the traffic, and Juli wondered how he could be so unaware she was attracted to him. She found Alan amazing. Funny and handsome. Kind and thoughtful. Everything she'd dreamed.

When they veered onto Highway 68, Juli caught on to the surprise as they inched down the road beside the Monterey County Fairgrounds. A billboard announced, MONTEREY BAY BLUES FESTIVAL.

She chuckled, and Alan glanced her way.

"That's sort of a giveaway," he said, motioning toward the sign. "I hope you like blues."

"I do, and I've never been to this festival."

"Then you're in for a treat."

He guided the car through the gate and found parking, and they headed into the fairgrounds, looking at the venue choices. Three stages had crowd-pleasing blues, and they settled at a bandstand, listening to the slow tempo of the melancholy music.

Alan slipped his arm across the back of her seat, and his fingers brushed her bare shoulder. The warmth radiated down her arm with a sensation too wonderful to put into words. She felt part of something special, and though she'd known Alan for only a short time, a sense of wholeness filled her. He was a believer, a man who understood God's love as she did.

With the sun beneath the horizon, Juli wrapped her sweater around her shoulders, and Alan snuggled closer, his arm lowering to add more warmth. The sky darkened, and she looked into the starry night toward a slender crescent moon. The music washed over her as Alan held her close.

"The sky's amazing," Alan whispered in her ear.

She felt a tickle against her skin. "I know. It's as lovely as the music."

"I'm looking at something even lovelier."

She lowered her gaze.

"I'm talking about you, Juli."

In the dark she could hide her blush. She couldn't remember being told she was lovely by anyone, except maybe her mother. "Thanks, but—"

"No buts. Please accept the compliment."

She could only nod and cling to the compliment as if it were a treasure. "This has been a great evening."

"I'm glad you took another chance on—"

She pressed her finger against his lips to silence him, and he kissed it. She drew her hand away, feeling the tingle of his touch. "We'll forget that first date. Let's pretend this is our first."

"I like that idea." He drew her closer. "We'll do this again, and soon."

She sent him a smile as big as the one in her heart. "I'd love to."

"But this time it'll be different. I don't like your driving alone at night. I'll pick you up."

"No. Please. I don't mind—"

This time his finger covered her lips. "Let me be a gentleman. I want to pick you up. We can do something in your area."

Like smell the garlic. Her spirit slumped. One day he'd have to visit her home and family. *Lord, help me get over this weirdness.*

"What's close to you?"

She drew up her shoulders. "Lots of places. Prunedale. Salinas. Let's talk details later."

His quizzical expression troubled her.

He tilted her chin upward. "But we've agreed it's a date, right?"

It's a date. She nodded, realizing she needed to get a grip on her hang-up. She had to learn to ignore the garlic jokes. She'd always been grateful she had dark hair because she felt so sorry for blonds, like Megan, who had to endure all the blond jokes. Megan didn't let them bother her. She laughed with the crowd while Juli felt bad for her. So why couldn't she be like Megan and laugh about garlic?

★

On Tuesday Alan headed across the hospital staff parking lot to his car. He'd come in early, and the day had weighed on him. Late afternoon sunlight spread through his tired body, and his stomach growled, reminding him he hadn't eaten in hours and that like Mother Hubbard's, his cupboard was bare. He needed to stop for some groceries.

Heat radiated from his car when he opened the door, and he climbed in and turned on the air then waited a moment for it to kick in. When the steering wheel felt cooler, he drove a short distance to the farmers' market held every Tuesday in Old Monterey. Alvarado Street was blocked from traffic so the vendors could sell their wares.

He parked near the conference center and headed along the main thoroughfare, eyeing the boutiques, book shops, and unique home furnishing stores until he reached the market, with the outdoor stands filled with produce and food specialties.

At the first stand he tossed a couple of lettuce heads into a bag; then he moved to another stand for broccoli, cauliflower, and a bundle of fresh spinach. As he selected his purchases, Juli entered his thoughts. He sensed she was holding back. Something troubled her about him or about herself. As much fun as they had together and as much as he cared about her, Juli's hesitation concerned him. Her "too many bad surprises" comment wouldn't leave his mind, and one day, if they were ever going to move ahead in their relationship, he would need to know what bothered her.

Forcing the worry from his mind, he focused on his shopping. He picked up a package of mushrooms, his favorite for salads and steak, and when he turned the corner, he could see a sign ahead for avocados. As he headed that way, he spotted a large sign, GARLIC GARDEN, and a woman who looked like Juli. He held back, watching until he knew for certain it was Juli. *Garlic Garden.* She'd said her father had a produce store. Garlic was produce, but she hadn't been specific.

Everything fell into place. His dislike of garlic—an allergy, he'd called it. This was her family's livelihood, and she'd been too embarrassed to tell him. Though her discomfort might seem silly to some, he knew how he felt about his career as a physician. He'd made a big deal to Tom about hiding it at the soup kitchen. He and Juli were both victims of their pasts, and they'd let the past affect their present, but not their future, he prayed. If he spoke to Juli here, catching her in the situation she'd tried to hide, he could embarrass her or worse. It wasn't worth the chance. He cared too much. He would let Juli tell him in her own good time. But if this was what bothered her so much, they needed to get it out in the open. He needed to be honest with her, too.

Foolish hang-ups.

So many things fell into place. Alan guessed Juli lived in Gilroy, garlic capital of the world. Was that why she'd been so hesitant to have him pick her up? Her father's owning a garlic store couldn't be all of it. The problem had to be deeper than that, and his curiosity rose. How many years had Juli allowed her past to hold her back from being the delightful person she was? She rarely dated, she'd said. She didn't recognize her attractiveness. She seemed so dedicated to giving that she didn't know how to receive.

Alan took a different route for the avocados, his mind spinning with questions. Perhaps her family was poor. That made sense. She was uncomfortable about his knowing that. She must have figured he had a good job at the hospital. How much money did a garlic store bring in? This whole thing couldn't stem from her father's garlic store.

Or could it?

six

Alan stood near the soup kitchen door and waited for Tom to catch up with him.

"I know I'm supposed to keep my mouth closed about the physician stuff," Tom said, rolling his eyes. "I still don't get you, pal."

"Trust me until I tell Juli myself. Please."

They passed through the doorway into the heat of the kitchen. Alan saw Juli and headed her way.

"Where's—"

Juli lifted her index finger toward the back door. Alan turned and saw Megan's blond hair and smiling face as she waved.

Tom nudged his shoulder. "Is that Juli's friend?"

"Sure is," Alan whispered.

"Wow!"

"Hi," Megan said, walking toward them, her gaze settling on Tom. "You're Tom." She extended her hand.

Tom grasped it. "And you're Megan. It's nice to meet you."

Juli took a step backward. "We'd better get to work before Bill squawks."

The foursome divided and found their workstations. Alan made a quick move to the cans of peaches. Today with the heat he could avoid the stoves and definitely the onions. He began opening lids, his mind sailing back to his great date with Juli the previous Saturday. Everything had gone well, except his discomfort when she'd asked about his family. He suspected she came from a poorer family, too, so it should be easy for him. Still, it wasn't. It was a time he wished he could forget, except it had instilled in him the values and character that made him the man he was today. When he felt confident Juli really cared about him, he'd tell her about his childhood poverty. He wanted no pity while dating.

When Alan got into the swing of filling dishes with peach slices, he scanned the kitchen and noticed Tom and Megan working together at a counter chopping vegetables. He could smell the aroma of chicken stock rising from the large soup kettles. When he looked Juli's way, she was watching him. He needed to dig deeper and see what made this wonderful woman tick.

The evening flew, and plans settled into his mind with the Fourth of July only two days away. When the food had been doled out, he watched Juli visiting with the homeless. Sometimes she knelt beside them, while other times she sat in an empty chair at the person's side. Alan listened and could hear the hope she offered them with her words of faith. When he noticed her take a young woman's hands, he moved closer.

"May I pray with you?" Juli asked.

The woman nodded, and Alan felt drawn to her side.

"Lord, bless Anne's efforts to reconcile with her family. Open their hearts to her needs and provide the light of forgiveness to touch them all. Jesus, You promise to be at our sides. Let Your light shine for Anne and her family. In Your name we pray. Amen."

"Amen," Alan added.

Juli raised her head in surprise. "Where did you come from?"

"I saw you praying and believe the more prayers, the better."

The young woman gave Alan a faint smile; then her eyes narrowed. "Haven't I seen you somewhere before?"

Her words triggered a memory. He felt nailed to the floor.

Recognition lit her face. "In emergency at the hospital. I had a knife wound and—"

Alan recollected too well. "I remember. How are you?"

"Fine, thanks to you. I only have a small scar between my ribs."

"You were blessed to have it nick the bone and not go any deeper."

Her expression said it all. "I know it could have gone into my heart."

Alan heard Juli's intake of breath.

"Praise the Lord," Juli said, reaching out to touch the girl's shoulder.

"Thanks so much," Anne said, knotting her hands in her lap. "To both of you. I wouldn't have survived without medical care, this food, or prayers. I've messed up my life, but I'm trying to make it better. Now if my family will give me a chance."

"Be confident, Anne. God is good, and He hears our prayers. I'll continue to pray that your family opens their hearts."

Tears welled in the young girl's eyes. "Thank you." She rose and looked as if she wanted to hug Juli, but she hesitated.

Juli stepped closer and embraced her without faltering. Her compassion and concern wrapped the girl in a healing balm, and Alan could only reiterate the prayer already sent up. *Lord, bless this girl. She needs Your help.*

Anne said good-bye and headed toward the door while Alan stood with Juli, his admiration increasing for Juli's ability to love and care about people. She truly followed God's instruction to live a life that emulated Jesus.

Before he could say anything, Megan headed their way with Tom close behind.

"We're going out for a bite to eat," Megan said. "Would you two like to join us?"

Alan looked at Juli but saw a no in her expression.

"I have a long day tomorrow, and I'm really tired tonight," Juli said. "I'd love to, but I should head home."

"What about Friday?" Alan asked, jumping into the conversation. "It's the Fourth. Would you like to go to the Monterey fireworks?"

A grin broke out on Tom's face. "I'd planned to ask Megan at the restaurant. What about it?"

"Sounds like fun." Megan turned to face Juli. "What do you think?"

Juli hesitated, and Alan felt his neck prickle.

"Well, I—"

"Idea," Megan burst in. "How about meeting at my place? Juli could spend the night with me. That'll save Alan the long ride to Gil—"

"What do you say?" Alan rested his hand on her shoulder.

"Say yes, Juli," Tom said. "Alan really likes you."

"That'll work," she said, a slight flush on her cheeks.

"Then it's a yes all the way around." Tom slipped his arm into Megan's. "See you on Friday." He and Megan turned away and headed out the door.

Alan stood beside Juli, wanting to press his hand against her rosy cheeks, but he knew she would be even more embarrassed. "Sorry for Tom's exuberance. I think he's doing a little matchmaking, too."

"I think so," she said, her flush fading. "Thanks so much for your prayers for Anne. She has such needs."

Alan knew more about Anne than he wanted to share. He nodded. "Let's hope God intervenes."

"She said a knife? How was she hurt?"

"An attempted robbery, sort of."

Juli's expression changed to a frown. "Robbery? But she doesn't have anything."

"A man owed her money for her services and didn't want to pay."

Juli lowered her gaze, and he sensed she understood. "Well, she's on the right road now. She told me how she'd been going to the church down the block. She realizes her sins, and she's asked God for forgiveness."

"Sometimes it takes us awhile to give up our foolish ways and let God take over. We drag a lot of baggage around with us."

"I know. It's time to put it in the Dumpster."

Alan realized Juli was referring to the baggage they'd talked about the other day. She needed to let it go.

And he needed to do the same.

‽

Juli looked out the window toward the road, waiting for Alan and Tom. Megan had given him directions to her apartment, and she hoped they had been clear. She grinned at her worrying.

"I guess I'm ready." Megan's voice cut into the silence.

Juli pivoted away from the window. "You look great," she said, admiring Megan's red, white, and blue knit top over walking shorts. Even her sandals were the colors of the American flag. Juli looked down at her coral capri pants with a navy and coral striped top and felt very unpatriotic. She should have thought of the holiday when she selected her outfit.

"You look good in—" Megan's attention flew to the window. "Here they are." She headed for the door.

Juli picked up her navy sweater and shoulder bag. "What about a sweater for tonight? It could be cold on the beach."

Megan released a giddy laugh. "I've got love to keep me warm."

Love? Juli tried to control her raised eyebrows. Megan hardly knew Tom. Megan flagged her through the doorway, and as Juli stepped outside, Alan opened the driver's door and met her. "You look wonderful."

She peered down at her outfit then at Megan's. "I forgot to look festive."

Alan slipped his arm around her back as he walked her to the car. "You look more than festive." He opened the passenger door.

She pondered his words as she slid into the seat. Behind her she saw Tom slide over while Alan held open the door for Megan. Megan gave Alan a smile as she joined Tom in the back. Alan closed her door then settled behind the wheel.

Juli noted that Tom hadn't moved to help Megan into the car. Alan had. His gentlemanly ways grew more wonderful each time she saw him.

He slipped his hand over hers. "You okay?"

"I'm fine." She managed a smile.

"Good. Buckle up, everyone. We're on our way."

She attached her seat belt as Alan backed down the driveway and pulled onto the highway. As he drove, Juli noticed most of the vehicles seemed to be headed toward the bay. The Fourth of July meant the beaches and parks would be filled. Alan maneuvered his way through the holiday traffic as the scenery became filled with celebration. Large flags flew from buildings, and children waved miniature ones as they bounded beside their parents. As they approached Fisherman's Wharf, the traffic came to a halt.

"It's good we came early," Alan said. "I thought we'd buy food on the wharf then sit on San Carlos Beach for the fireworks."

No reply came from the backseat.

"Or we could go to Colton Hall," he added. "They have food there, plus music."

Juli glanced over her shoulder, waiting to hear what Tom and Megan preferred to do, but then spun forward after seeing them in a deep kiss that embarrassed her. Megan barely knew Tom, and that kind of familiarity seemed terribly inappropriate.

"The wharf sounds fun," she said, managing to control her uneasiness. "We'll want to find a place on the beach early anyway."

He slipped his hand over hers. "Right. We want a good spot for the fireworks."

She rolled her hand upward beneath his, wove her fingers through his, and gave them a squeeze.

Alan's face lit with a smile that brightened his eyes, and Juli smiled back, sensing the same light in her eyes.

A horn tooted behind them, and the traffic began to move. "Finally," Alan said as he released her hand and gripped the steering wheel.

Juli watched him concentrate on the traffic, relishing the memory of his fingers on hers.

"Look at this traffic," Tom said.

Juli assumed they'd finally come up for air. The image of them set her on edge. She hoped they'd manage to harness their affection at the wharf.

When they arrived, Alan parked, and Juli stepped out into the warm bay breeze. The unique scent filled her senses—bay water, fish, and warm sand. As they neared the wharf, new aromas of food drifted on the air.

Megan and Tom walked ahead, talking with their faces close, their hands clasped together. Juli liked hand-holding and wished Alan was holding hers. He walked beside her, his arm brushing against hers, his fingers only inches away. Juli knew she and Alan weren't in love, but she'd felt a strong interest that had grown into attraction, and she'd thought it was reciprocated. A picture rose in her mind—Tom and Megan kissing in the backseat. Alan had never asked to kiss her, never tried. Men and women sometimes had platonic friendships. She hoped Alan's feelings had grown deeper than that.

They passed the weathered FISHERMAN'S WHARF sign and wove their way through the crowd toward the pink building sporting a bright blue lighthouse. They passed Harbour House and shops selling silver, pearls, T-shirts, and artwork. Tangy aromas drifted from the restaurants—seafood, steak, Mexican spices. Tom headed for the Casa Carmelkorn shop, but Alan whistled and cupped his hands over his mouth to form a megaphone. "Let's eat dinner first."

Tom sauntered back with Megan's hand woven in his. "I'm ready." He turned to Megan. "I'll pick up some caramel corn to take to the beach."

Megan nestled against his shoulder as they discussed their restaurant options—Crabby Jim's, Captain's Gig Restaurant with its covered porch for outdoor eating, and Cabo's Wild Mexican Seafood. They walked to the end of the wharf and back, eyeing the possibilities, and eventually agreed on Café Fina. They returned to the butter-colored clapboard building and went inside. The air-conditioning felt great to Juli, and she was pleased to see the broad windows offered a sweeping view of the harbor.

Juli listened to the conversation, the romantic tones of Tom and Megan and Alan's witty comments. She perused the menu, especially the wood grill fare of chicken and veal dishes. She noticed the New York steak and wondered if that would be Alan's choice. When Megan mentioned that Café Fina's pasta was homemade, Juli settled on Italian sausage with fettuccini.

"Sounds good," Alan said, "but I'll take the Pasta Fina. It has baby bay shrimp, Roma tomatoes, and onions covered in clam butter sauce."

The waitress wrote down their orders, and Juli turned to the window and watched the sun lowering in the sky. Its golden hues spread across the bay like deep yellow oil on water floating along the top, creating a vibrant splash of color.

"You're quiet," Alan said, leaning closer. He glanced at the other two, and Juli followed his direction. Seeing they were preoccupied, Alan leaned closer. "Are you upset with me about something?"

Her pulse tripped. "No. Not at all. I'm just distracted, I guess."

Alan tilted his head toward Tom and Megan. "You're surprised about—"

He didn't continue, but she knew what he meant.

She gave a faint shrug. "A little."

He nodded as if understanding.

She felt his fingers brush against her lower arm, a touch

so gentle it sent a tingle to her heart. She felt her pulse give a jig, and it left her confounded. She longed to know how Alan really felt about her. Did he think of her as a friend, a girlfriend, a date, a what?

Letting the question slide, Juli managed to be chattier. She and Alan talked about the soup kitchen, past Fourth of July experiences, and the ambience of the restaurant, anything to help her avoid watching Tom and Megan. Occasionally one of them added a comment, but the conversation tended to be hers and Alan's until finally the food arrived.

They quieted and concentrated on their meals. They skipped dessert and ordered coffee, letting time pass as the sunlight turned to dusk and the lights came up on the wharf. The crowd thickened, and they discussed the need to find a spot on the beach. Alan motioned for the bill. When they stepped outside, he and Tom agreed to run back to the car for blankets while Megan went for the caramel corn and Juli headed for Carousel Candies to pick up some sweets.

Inside the store she made her purchase—and faced the truth. She really liked Alan, and if they were going to get anywhere, she had to stop her worries. She had to do something to get rid of her ridiculous attitude about Gilroy and garlic. She needed to give her concerns to the Lord and let Him guide her. Juli knew she had to take a leap of faith, to step outside her comfort zone, but she sensed that was what the Lord would have her do.

When they reached the crowded beach, they found a spot and spread their blankets close to the water. With the lack of sun and a breeze from the bay, a chill had settled over the sand. Megan and Tom stretched out on their blanket, arms wrapped around each other, while Alan and Juli sat Indian-style. She reached for her sweater tied to the strap of her shoulder bag, and Alan helped her slip it on then stretched out his legs and patted the blanket between his knees. "Come over here. We might as well stay warm."

She looked at his face in the dim light. "Are you sure?"

"Am I sure? I insist."

His voice rang with good humor.

"Want a piece of candy first?" She pulled a small package from her shoulder bag.

He shook his head. "You're sweet enough for me."

The look in his eyes sent her heart on a wild ride. She scooted across the blanket and settled down with her back against his torso. Alan wrapped his arms around her and rested his chin on her shoulder. "Now isn't that much better?"

Better. It was wonderful to be so close yet show good taste. "It's much, much better, but are you comfortable?"

"I'm very comfortable. Isn't that like you to be concerned about people?"

His words settled over her. "Is it bad to be so concerned?"

"Juli, it's what the Lord expects. How can you ask? It's what makes me care about you so much."

She stopped herself from asking him to define "care about you." She decided to enjoy his words and leave the situation in God's hands.

Music from the wharf drifted down to the beach, and they sat without talking and watched people wander along the bay searching for a place to sit. She loved the feel of Alan's arms embracing her and keeping her warm. It reminded her of the Bible verse in Ecclesiastes that began, "Two are better than one," and went on to say, "But how can one keep warm alone?" The beautiful words that defined a loving relationship hung in her mind. *Two are better than one.*

Tom and Megan were lip-locked again. Juli averted her gaze, and Alan gave her a firm squeeze.

"I know that bothers you," he whispered in her ear. "It bothers me, too."

Juli turned, her mouth close to his. "They don't know each other that well."

"I know."

She saw something in his eyes, and butterfly wings revisited her heart until she nearly lost her breath. "They just met," she was finally able to say.

She saw his lips move, and she felt them brush the end of her nose. The sweetness of his kiss washed over her. She loved that so much more than tempting herself to sin. Too much passion too soon wasn't what the Lord expected, and it wasn't what she expected.

Alan's gaze sought hers, and she smiled to let him know she loved his kiss. She felt his shoulders relax, and she turned again to face the water, nestling inside the circle of his arms. Tonight she knew why he'd never tried to kiss her. Alan respected her, and he'd waited for her permission to move forward. She needed to decide what she wanted, and if she wanted Alan, she needed to be honest with him. So many things piled up in her mind.

A hiss and a bang charged the sky, and a burst of color shot through the night, with red, white, and blue fairy dust floating downward to the water.

"That surprised you," Alan said, nuzzling his chin against her shoulder.

Another burst lit the darkness like a golden chrysanthemum followed by tiny pinwheels spiraling through the air. The crowd responded with applause and cheers.

Juli watched one display after another, each more beautiful than the last, bursts in the shape of hearts and stars, fountains of brilliant color, but she realized the glorious glow held nothing to the light in her heart. The Lord had sent her a man who respected her and cared about her, a gift greater than any fireworks display on earth.

seven

Juli's voice rose in song as the words to one of her favorite praise hymns flashed on the screen, "Lord, We Lift Your Name on High." The words and tune rang in her heart. Her father's deep bass voice rumbled beside her, while her mother's softer tone blended with the others nearby. Juli lifted her hand, grateful to belong to an active congregation and to have Christian parents.

The thought skittered down her back. They were great parents, but they knew how to pull her strings, and lately she felt tied by their expectations. The problem had really been her dad. He seemed bound to old traditions, and though she loved him deeply, sometimes she resented his expectations. Alan had drawn out her earlier desire to help people, to be a counselor or social worker. While she honored God by following her father's wishes, her own desires had fallen by the wayside.

A few years ago her father had wanted a family member in the store, so she took over, releasing her mother from the day-to-day work there, but now the store had prospered. They had trusted employees. Why did he still need her there every day? The question charged through her like a volt of energy. She'd never really thought of it that way before.

Lord, is that what You want for me? The question niggled her. She knew that if God had a new course for her to follow, she would sense it. The Spirit would guide her. She believed something would happen to make her know for sure that she was following God's will.

The congregation sat, and Juli followed, opening her Bible to the verse the pastor had stated, Romans 12:6. As he began to speak, Juli held her breath.

" 'We have different gifts, according to the grace given us,' "
he read from scripture.

Different gifts. Juli closed her eyes, knowing God had given
her a gift. Alan had spoken of her gifts often, and so had
others. Juli's pulse skipped as she listened.

" 'If it is serving, let him serve; if it is teaching, let him teach;
if it is encouraging, let him encourage; if it is contributing to
the needs of others, let him give generously.' "

God's Word settled into her mind. Serving. Encouraging.
Contributing to the needs of others. Wasn't that what she
wanted to do with her life? The pastor's words wrapped
around her senses as she slipped into her own thoughts. What
had her life become? Keeping books, writing up orders, doing
inventory, waiting on customers who bought garlic braids,
garlic mustard, garlic pasta sauce, garlic salsa, and garlic bread.
Pickled and roasted garlic. Garlic in jars, cans, shakers, and
fresh. Garlic peelers, presses, and slicers. Is that what the Lord
expected of her when her heart yearned to serve others?

"Listen to God's words," the pastor said.

Juli's thoughts faded.

" 'Honor one another above yourselves. Never be lacking in
zeal, but keep your spiritual fervor, serving the Lord.' Each of
us can walk our own path, but we are challenged to use the
gifts given to us by the Holy Spirit by honoring others above
ourselves."

Tears welled in Juli's eyes. *Lord, is that what You want for
me?* God had answered her question in an amazing way, and
she couldn't wait to talk with Alan. He seemed to understand.
He'd encouraged her, and before she spoke to her parents, she
wanted to digest what she'd heard today.

The sermon had ended, and they stood as prayers rose for
the needs of others. Juli managed to quiet her excitement and
concentrate on the petitions. The music began, and voices
lifted in praise as high as Juli's heart had raised at her amazing
awareness. God wanted His children to use their gifts, and

she was sure hers didn't involve managing a garlic store.

Now all she had to do was convince her parents.

ed

"Why so quiet?"

Her mother's voice edged into Juli's thoughts. She shifted on the family room sofa and saw her mother's face filled with questions. "I was thinking about the sermon."

Her mother smiled. "I thought maybe you had a problem."

Juli grinned but didn't respond; if she said she didn't, it would have been a lie. She set her feet firmly on the floor and leaned forward. "What are your gifts, Mom?"

"My gifts?"

"Gifts of the Spirit. From the sermon."

Her mother waved her hand in the air as if she were brushing away cobwebs. "The Bible says we're given gifts according to God's grace. Who's to say some of those gifts aren't being a mother and a wife? I believe those are my gifts."

Juli shook her head. "That's not an easy job, Mom. If you break it down into parts, you've been a teacher, nurturer, nursemaid to Jim and me, and business partner to Dad."

"I'm no such thing. Your father is the businessman."

"Don't wave away your gifts as if they're not important." She looked at the carpet, trying to pose the right question. "Did you ever want something more? Something deeper?"

Her mother tilted her head upward as if looking for the answer on the ceiling. "I had childhood dreams but nothing that meant anything."

"Really? What kind of dreams?"

"Children want to be nurses and firemen, the typical things, you know."

Juli chuckled. "So you wanted to be a fireman?"

Her mother laughed. "No, I wanted to be a nurse."

"A nurse." Juli realized her mother's dream and hers had similar purposes—to help others become well. "What happened?"

"What happened?" She shook her head. "Marriage, Jim and you. That's what happened."

Her mother's words kicked at Juli's heart. "So you gave up a dream because you got married and had kids. Did you ever resent us, Mom?" Looking into her mother's startled eyes, Juli wished she could have retracted the question.

"How can you ask me that? You and Jim mean everything to me. I wouldn't have given you up for a hundred nurses' uniforms. In fact, they don't even wear regular nurses' uniforms anymore. They wear little smocks. Not even a hat."

Her response made Juli chuckle again. "Then definitely it wasn't worth it," Juli said, making light of her question.

Sinking back into the easy chair, her mother released a sigh. "To be honest, sometimes I wonder how it would have been to have my own career and come home, knowing I'd helped someone regain their health. But then I'd think of you and your brother, and I realized this was where God wanted me to be. I've raised two wonderful children I've always been proud of. That's a parent's real dream."

"Children I've always been proud of." The words fell like a weight on Juli's shoulders. Would her mother be proud if she decided to strike out on her own after living at home and working in the family business? She couldn't look into her mother's eyes for fear her quandary glowed like a neon sign on her forehead.

She slapped her hands against her knees and rose. "I'd better get home. Tell Daddy I said good-bye. The last I saw him, he was taking a nap in the living room recliner."

"That's his gift," her mother said with a twinkle in her eyes.

Juli laughed and headed toward the doorway. "Thanks for Sunday dinner, Mom. It was great as usual." She waved over her head and didn't look back.

When she stepped onto the veranda and took the stairs to her own apartment, Juli's head spun with their conversation. Every Sunday she had dinner with her parents. Every Monday she went to work in the store. Her life had seemed like a broken record for so long until Alan had entered it, and now she didn't want to hear the same repetitive tune. She wanted to hear the rest of the symphony.

She headed into her bedroom and stretched out on the bed, watching the sunlight dance on the ceiling. She'd come to realize her pulse also did a jig when she spent time with Alan. Since Friday, images of the evening filled her. The fireworks erupting overhead like colorful flowers provided an amazing backdrop to the blossoming emotion of being with Alan. She remembered the solidness of his chest supporting her as they watched the brilliant display, his chin nestling against her shoulder. The sweet memory rolled over her like silk. She could still recall his lips brushing against her nose in that tender kiss. He meant so much to her, and she feared for her heart, despite her longing to feel confident and trust Alan.

She pressed her palms against her temple, trying to hold back the uneasy feelings that stomped over her confidence and caused her to question herself. If she could learn to believe in herself, she would be more fulfilled. This meant she had to stop doubting what Jesus said and what He could do. He came into the world to give believers an abundant life. Abundant life meant ample, full, a fulfilled life, didn't it?

In the distance Juli heard her telephone ring. With Alan still on her mind, she hurried to answer it, but she covered her disappointment when she heard a different voice on the line.

"Hi, Megan."

Megan went on and on about her Saturday night date with Tom, and though Juli had enjoyed the wonderful Friday night with Alan, she felt envious. Alan hadn't called her or asked her out for Saturday evening.

"I'm glad you had so much fun," Juli said, keeping her voice as bright as she could.

"I think I'm falling in love, Juli."

Love? Juli felt the air leave her lungs. "Megan, you said that on Friday. Please be careful. You've only known Tom a short time. Love is something that has to grow. Love and passion aren't the same."

"What does that mean?"

Juli bit her lip, realizing she'd opened up a touchy subject. "Passion is arousing desire in the body, but love is a deep emotion that moves the heart and soul."

"This is more than passion. He does move my heart."

Juli cringed at the upset tone of Megan's voice. "I'm sor—"

"Just because we kiss a little doesn't mean we don't talk and have a good time."

Kiss a little. Juli bit her tongue to avoid saying her thoughts. "Those long kisses can lead to—"

"Long kisses. What were you doing, watching us?"

Juli's back stiffened. "Megan, I turned around to ask you a question, and you were. . . I don't know. I turned away to give you privacy, but what I saw didn't look like a little kiss to me."

"From what I can see, you and Alan don't do anything."

Her comment smacked Juli, but she figured it was Megan's defensiveness. The word *respect* bounded to her tongue, but she swallowed it. "I believe in taking things slow, and so does Alan."

"You two seem to be at a dead stop, in my opinion."

The line went silent until Megan's soft sob came over the wire.

"Megan, are you okay? I'm really sorry. I know I should be happy for you, but—"

"It's not you." Her voice broke with another sob. "It's me, Juli."

"You? What do you mean?"

"I'm rushing things, I know. I talk to you about God, and then I forget what I should do. I know I need to be careful. Tom told me he's been footloose for a long time, and you've just reminded me of that. Do you think he's trying to use me?"

"I hope not, Megan, but you're aware of that. Remember that passion is the body's physical reaction. Love comes from the heart."

Juli heard only silence.

"Megan?"

"I'm here. I know. I really like him, and I want things to work out."

"Pray about it. You told me to listen to the Lord awhile ago. You do the same. You can't go wrong." She heard Megan chuckle.

"I guess I should heed my own advice."

"Can we forget this happened? I didn't want to hurt you."

"I know. You're being a good friend, and I'm sorry for what I said. I didn't mean it."

When the call ended, Megan's words hung in Juli's thoughts. She'd heard judges tell the jury to disregard testimony, but Juli figured once they'd heard it, they'd heard it. She and Megan had both said things that had hurt the other, but they'd ended the conversation with advice that made sense.

Juli sank onto her living room sofa, thinking about Megan and Tom and then Alan. The call had made her appreciate Alan even more. He respected her, and that was a tremendous gift. She prayed Megan would listen to the Lord, and Juli knew she should, too.

Before she could think any more, the telephone rang, and this time she knew it was Alan.

❧

When Alan heard Juli's voice, he realized something was wrong. "You sound upset. What's up?"

She hesitated and then told him what had transpired.

"I feel the same way, Juli," Alan said, hoping to reassure her they were on the same page. "Tom isn't a guy to last long with a woman, and I'm afraid Megan trusts him and what he's saying, and—" He stopped himself, realizing he should keep this to himself. How could he judge Tom? "Let's see what happens.

Maybe one day Tom will change." He heard Juli's intake of breath.

"I think she understands now. At least I hope so. And you know what she told me?"

"What?"

"Tom admitted to her that he liked to play the field."

"Really? That's a good sign. Tom doesn't usually admit that to himself."

"We can pray that Tom cares enough to change and Megan uses wisdom. I have to leave it to the Lord."

Listening to Juli's voice as she worried about her friend touched him. Juli had captivated him with her concern for others, but he worried that she overlooked her own needs. He wished he could draw out all the hidden things in her heart. Then maybe he could open up more about his own. They needed to have time alone when they weren't surrounded by other people.

A smile lingered in his heart. "I wish I hadn't needed to work the past two days. Twelve-hour shifts can be so long. I miss you."

"I miss you, too. I wish we had time to talk. Alone, I mean. Wednesday is always too difficult."

Alan drew back, pleased to hear what he'd just thought. "How about tomorrow? I'm off. Let's do something different."

"Like parasailing?"

He heard laughter in her voice. "Sure, why not?"

"I'm even nervous on a ladder. That's why not."

He chuckled with her. "Do you have a bicycle?"

"A bicycle? I have an ancient one. I haven't been on it in years."

"Then it's time to dust it off and have some fun. What do you say?"

"Biking?" She paused. "Okay, but I hope I can still remember how to keep my balance."

He grinned. "Maybe we should rent a bicycle built for two."

"I wouldn't put you through that. Where do you want to go?"

"I don't care. Up your way. I'll pick you up, and we can—"

"How about the old Fort Ord bicycle trails? That's nearly halfway for both of us, and we'll have a beautiful view of the bay."

His shoulders drooped. "You want to meet again, Juli. That's so frust—"

"I'll take the day off, and we can get started earlier. I'll save you all the time of driving here, and I'd love to go to Marina Dunes Beach. It's beautiful and quiet."

He gave up. She'd been holding her secret back for too long, but so had he, and it all seemed so foolish. "We can sit on the beach and talk there. I'll bring a blanket."

After they'd made plans and he'd hung up, Alan lowered his head, facing his own quandary. He should have been up front with Juli from the beginning about his work. He'd never told her he was a physician to prevent a slip-up at the soup kitchen, but now he'd dragged it on so long it would be shocking to her, and she'd be disappointed in him that he hadn't been open with her. She hadn't either, but that didn't excuse him.

He buried his face in his hands, realizing he always expected the worst to happen. For so many years he'd prayed for things to be better in his life, and they seemed to get worse. When blessings came, he waited for them to fade away again, just as they had in the past. Juli had become one of those blessings, and he feared losing her. He longed to develop a healthy relationship with her, and that meant they both had to be open and trusting. *Lord, help me trust Juli and trust You. You promise good things for those who wait and those who put their confidence in You. You know my needs, and I pray for Your guidance.*

⁂

The warm breeze fluttered through Juli's hair, and perspiration beaded along her forehead. Her old bicycle hadn't been that bad once she cleaned it up, and even though it wasn't a mountain bike like Alan's, they managed to stay together as they soared along the bike trails on the old Fort Ord land. Horses, hiking, and biking had returned this discarded army base to a valuable piece of land that offered enjoyment to many.

She pumped harder as Alan moved farther ahead. "Going to a fire?" she called. The wind carried her voice behind her, but she knew Alan heard because he glanced over his shoulder and sent her a teasing smile. He slowed then grinned when she reached him.

"We're not too far from the pedestrian access to the beach. I got carried away."

Juli knew he was holding back for her. "I know the way. I'll meet you there."

He didn't refuse. His long, muscular legs gained momentum, and she watched him shoot ahead then vanish down an incline. She slowed, catching her breath and admiring the wonderful view. The amazing silvery blue water rolled in white foam to pale sand, colors so muted they looked surreal in the summer sun. Above a baby blue sky spread a misty haze that lay over the foothills in the distance. The scene was breathtaking and inspiring, and her enthusiasm rose. Today she wanted to open her heart and share her dreams with Alan.

When the beach access came into sight, she veered downward toward the lake and climbed from the bike. The nearly empty beach seemed to be a splendor hidden from the world. The miles of sand and surf offered them solitude. Alan had spread a blanket at the foot of a sand dune, and her feet sank into the crystals as she made her way to his side.

He pointed to the sky, where a hang glider drifted above, his sail adding a splash of color to the pastel surroundings. "It's gorgeous," she said, sinking to the blanket.

Alan unzipped a backpack. "I brought a treat."

He pulled out two cans of soda and a cylinder of potato chips.

Juli popped open the soda tab and took a long drink then reached for a small stack of chips from the container. She nibbled on them, took another drink then leaned back on one elbow and admired Alan's summer glow.

"You look so healthy."

"I've been trying to jog a little every day. Working long hours inside a hospital isn't good for a tan."

Neither was working at the Garlic Garden. "This is a good day, Alan. We're so rarely alone, and I've been doing a lot of thinking. I could really bounce some thoughts off someone."

"Bounce away."

He joined her on the blanket, his legs extended, leaning on one hip and propped on his elbow.

Juli adjusted herself and sat up with her legs crossed in front of her. "I know this is nothing new, but it is to me in a way. We talked before about my interest in social work and my lack of college."

"I hope I didn't cause you to feel that not having a college degree made you inferior."

"No. It wasn't that at all. I've looked into my own heart and realize I've pushed away my dream for fear of upsetting my parents, but yesterday in church some things struck me, and now I'm so confused."

"What happened yesterday?" He pulled his knees upward and scooted to a seated position beside her.

"God's Word." Juli shared the message she'd heard and the verses that had caused her new thoughts. "The verses about how God gives each of us different gifts. The one that really hit me was 'If it is contributing to the needs of others, let him give generously.'"

"You do give generously. Every time I see you with people at the soup kitchen, I admire you. Even though I work with people dealing with health issues, I'm too consumed with getting them better and not even thinking about their emotional needs. I need to work on that."

"But God's given me that gift, and couldn't I use it better in a field like social work or counseling? That's why I'm confused. Am I just falling back on an empty dream that should stay where it is?"

"I told you the other day you should use your talents to the fullest. Certainly you could be of greater service working with people dealing with problems."

Juli nodded, feeling emotion lump in her throat. "I want to do what God wants me to do. That's all I can say. Starting college at my age seems—"

"Your age?" Alan chuckled. "Juli, you're twenty-five."

"I'll be twenty-six in September, and I couldn't go full-time. I need money to live on, so it would take forever."

"You work for your dad. Maybe you could work full-time in the summer and fall when the produce is harvested and then work part-time in the spring and winter so you can go to school full-time. That would speed up schooling."

"That's what I need to hear. Practical ways to approach the problem. That's a great idea. I wouldn't have to dump everything on my dad all at once. I don't want to upset them."

Alan slid his arm around her shoulder. "I can't image your parents not supporting something you want so badly."

Her pulse gave a kick. Alan didn't know her parents. They were good people, but the focus had always been on being a good Christian and on the garlic business. She'd fallen into their needs so easily. "You'll have to meet them to understand."

Alan frowned.

"You don't want to meet them?"

"No, it's not that. I'd love to meet them, but I guess I don't understand your relationship with them."

"That's the paradox. I love them, but I feel bound to them." Her eyes blurred again. "I sound like a teenager trying to break loose from the proverbial apron strings. That's really what my problem is. I've never cut the ties and struck out on my own. I don't even know that I could."

Alan rose and reached toward her. She placed her hand in his as he helped her stand, and he drew her into his arms. She rested her head against his chest and savored his support. Alan gave her courage to take steps forward, and she knew God had blessed her with this friendship.

"You can do anything you want, Juli," Alan whispered in her ear. "With God all things are possible. You know that."

"I do," she murmured against his T-shirt. "I just need to remember it."

He drew her closer, and she stood beside him feeling the wind ruffle her hair and hearing the sound of the surf. She'd let so many things hold her back, and today she knew it was time to step forward and make her life different.

She drew her head back to look into his face. "Would you really like to meet my parents?"

"Absolutely."

"I'll invite you to dinner. You can see where I live, and we'll go down later and meet them."

"I couldn't be happier."

"You're kidding, right?"

He grinned. "I thought you lived in a tent and didn't want me to know."

She chuckled. "Sorry to disappoint you. I really live in a nice apartment in"—she needed to be trusting and honest—"in Gilroy."

"Gilroy." He let out a laugh. "You mean the gar—"

"The garlic capital of the world." The situation struck her as funny, and she laughed. Laughing about it felt so much better than the irritation that rankled her so often. She lifted her eyes to the clear blue heavens and sent up a grateful thank-You.

eight

"Wait up."

Alan halted and turned in Tom's direction. He waved then waited for him to catch up.

Tom strode to his side and grinned. "You have a bounce to your step. What's up?"

"I'm off tomorrow."

"Not me. I have to work. I hate working the full weekend. Sunday's supposed to be a day of rest." He gave Alan a grin, as if wanting him to know he knew what God said in the Bible. "Any plans for the weekend?"

"Juli invited me to her house for dinner. I've never been there."

"You're kidding."

"No. She takes her time, and I don't mind that."

Tom winked. "I hope not too much time."

Alan didn't like the sound of his comment. "Just right for me. She's perfect."

"So is Megan. I'm seeing her again tonight. She's quite a woman."

"I've noticed." The words flew from his mouth before he could stop them.

Tom faltered. "What does that mean?"

Alan tensed, wondering how much to say, but he felt compelled. "You two seem to have dived right into a pretty heavy relationship."

Tom chuckled. "Jealous?"

Alan shook his head. "Not at all. My dating style is different."

"Different?" Tom stopped. "In what way?"

"I like to know a woman before I get carried away, and even then I want to respect her."

Tom drew up his shoulders. "Listen. I respect Megan, and I was honest with her, and I really do care about her a lot. Anyway, she knows what she's doing."

Alan wondered if Megan really did know. "I mean respect in a biblical sense." He placed his hand on Tom's arm. "I've heard you mention the Bible. Are you a believer?"

Tom's eyes widened. "I believe. . .I believe in God, but I'm not a churchgoer if that's what you mean. I know Jesus died for my sins, but—"

Alan waited, hoping he'd continue. "But what, Tom?"

"I don't know. If I sin a little, then I'm forgiven. Right?"

"You'd better start reading that Bible instead of talking about it. You need to be sorry for your sins and repent."

Tom looked away, his head drooping.

"I don't want to judge you, Tom, and I think what you do is between you and God, but I also think it can lead to trouble."

"Trouble? You mean you're afraid she'll get preg—"

"I'm talking about friendship." Alan struggled to keep the shock from his face. "To me, an intimate relationship means commitment. I can't make a commitment until I know someone's heart and soul."

Tom kicked a stone with the toe of his shoe. "I'm not stupid, Alan. I'm not going to get either one of us in trouble."

"You're missing the point, but it's your life. Yours and Megan's. I think too much of Juli to use her."

"Use her?"

"I haven't even kissed Juli on the mouth, Tom. Not that I don't want to, but I'm giving it time. I want her to know that when I do, it means something."

Tom held up his hand like a traffic cop. "Stop right there. I'm not looking for marriage. I'm looking for a good time."

Alan shook his head. "That's my point. What about Megan? Maybe she expects more."

"I suppose you'll open your big mouth to Juli about this."

"It's your business. You lead your life the way you want. I just wanted you to know Juli and I were both uncomfortable last Friday with you two carrying on in the backseat. I'd like you to respect Juli at least."

"Sorry." He gave another stone a quick kick, and it skidded across the pavement. "I'll make sure we drive separate cars next time."

At least Tom would keep his hands on the steering wheel, Alan hoped. "I don't want to argue with you over this. I'm just letting you know I've thought it over, and I wanted to let you know how I feel."

"Consider it done," Tom said, stuffing his hands into his pockets. "See you Monday."

Alan watched him stride away and knew he'd caused stress between them, but he cared about Juli, and he knew she'd been ill at ease the week before. So had he. All he could do was hope that what he said might give Tom something to think about.

❧

Juli stared into her refrigerator, eyeing the pork chops. Not only had she invited Alan to her house, but she'd also invited him for dinner. What was she thinking? She usually had Sunday dinner with her parents, and once she told them she was having company, her mother was all over her for details. She thought by the time she'd reached her midtwenties they would see her as an adult, but she had been totally mistaken. Her father still called her his little girl.

She released a stream of breath and pulled the chops from the refrigerator. She planned to bake them in the oven. The oven heat came to mind. Today was too beautiful to turn it on. She'd barbeque, but that meant going into the yard, and her parents would be out there in a flash, probing Alan with questions. All she'd planned to do was drop by for a minute and introduce him to her parents.

For the hundredth time Juli realized she needed to move to her own apartment. She sank into a kitchen chair, knowing the convenience of living close to her work, but—

But what? If she had her own place, she wouldn't feel so hemmed in. What did Alan think of her still living at home, even if it was separate from her parents' part of the house? She could only imagine.

"Why did I invite him?" The words sounded in her ears and surprised her. She glanced at the clock, knowing she needed to start cooking. He'd be here soon.

Juli rose, returned to the kitchen, and opened the cabinet. She would make pork chops in mushroom soup. They were always tender and formed wonderful gravy. Alan would be impressed. After searching for a few fruitless moments, she realized she'd used her last can of the soup. Drawing up her shoulders, she opened the door to the outside walkway, followed the stairs to the first floor, and stepped into the foyer.

"Mom?"

The scent of home-baked bread filled the air along with the sweet aroma of something else.

Her mother's distant voice greeted her. "I'm in the kitchen."

She followed the lengthy foyer past the staircase, through the family room, and into the kitchen, where her mother stood beside the oven.

"Mom, it's too hot to bake."

"We have air-conditioning." She turned to greet Juli. "You know your father and his homemade bread, and I couldn't resist trying this new cake recipe."

"It smells wonderful." Seeing her mother's eager look, she knew the cake was probably her favorite.

"It's poppy seed cake with lemon zest. Your favorite."

She grasped her courage. "Remember, Mom—I told you I'm having company for dinner today."

"I know, but maybe you could bring your friend here for

dessert." She gave Juli a broad smile.

Juli's stomach did a slow dive. "We'll come down after dinner for a minute."

Her mother faced her, waving an oven mitt that looked like a pig puppet. "What are you serving?"

The coincidence nearly made her laugh. "Pork chops, but I need to borrow a can of mushroom soup."

"Pork chops and mushroom soup? On Sunday?" She waved her pig puppet–encased hand again.

"It'll be good. The chops are so tender."

"Is Megan coming over?"

"No."

Her mother stood in front of her, waiting.

Juli looked at the pattern of the tile floor and exhaled. "It's a person I met at the soup kitchen."

Her mother's eyes widened. "It's not—"

"Mom, it's not one of the homeless, although that would be a very kind and Christian thing to do. Doesn't Jesus tell us to—"

"I'm sorry, Juli." She pulled off the oven mitt. "I know that some of the people have problems and—"

"It's one of the volunteers."

"Well, that's easy. Invite her to eat with us. That makes perfect sense."

Juli's heartbeat kicked up a notch. "Him."

"We always like to meet your fri—" Her mother's gaze focused on her. "Him?"

Juli put her hands on her hips. "Don't sound so shocked."

Her mother began to laugh. "Juli, you so rarely date that I am shocked, but pleasantly so. Your father and I have been worried you'll end up not finding a husband. You know the Lord said—"

"I know what the Lord said. It's not good that man should be alone." She tried to make her voice lighthearted. "But the Bible doesn't say anything about women."

"Juliana. Don't you make jokes about—"

"Mom, I'm sure God knows I'm joking. Don't you think He has a sense of humor?"

"Well. . . ," her mother sputtered. "No matter, I'm sure your father would like to meet your friend. Please invite him to dinner. I'm making pasta, and we have the homemade bread and the cake." She gestured to the oven. "Please."

Juli swallowed, anticipating her mother's response to her next question. "Are you using garlic?"

"Garlic? I always use garlic in pasta."

"Alan has an aversion to garlic. It's best we—"

"You won't even know it's there. I'll only put in a drop. How's that?"

Juli held up her hand to stop her mother's pleading. "I'll ask him, Mom, but if he seems uneasy, I'll cook as planned. I'm sorry, but I wasn't thinking about it being Sunday when I invited him."

Her mother's gaze dropped. "Okay. I can't ask any more of you."

She could, but Juli hoped she wouldn't. "Do you have a can of cream of mushroom soup I can borrow?" She eyed her mother's face. "Just in case."

Her mother opened the small kitchen pantry, pulled out a can, and handed it to Juli. "Here."

"Thanks, Mom." She leaned closer and kissed her cheek then stepped back. "Where's Dad?"

"He was reading the Sunday paper in the living room, but I'll guess if you check, he'll be sleeping."

Juli took a step backward. "I won't bother him, then." She inched closer to the door. "I'll call you after Alan gets here. Okay?"

"Okay." Her voice didn't convince Juli that it really was okay, but her mom was apparently trying to be agreeable.

Easing past the living room, Juli peeked inside and saw her dad tipped back in the recliner, an open newspaper ready to fall to the floor, his eyeglasses skewed to one side from the tilt of his head. She grinned and slipped outside.

As she darted up the stairs, the image of her mother's face hung in her memory. She didn't want the day to be stressful, but she'd told Alan she would introduce him, and she would. Juli wondered how Alan would react to her parents and then wondered what they would think of him.

Inside, she faced her refrigerator then tossed her hands in the air and sat on a kitchen chair. If Alan didn't want to eat with her parents, she would get creative. She wasn't sure what that meant, but that's what she would have to do.

❧

Alan turned onto Wildrose Court, amazed at the homes. With Juli's reticence to let him pick her up, he'd suspected Juli's parents were hardworking people without a lot of finances, but the surrounding area gave him another perspective. Expensive two-story estates sprawled among rolling hills, pastel-painted stuccos and dark-stained homes with windows that opened to a grand view of the green fields in the valley.

When he spotted Juli's address, he put on the brake and sat a moment, wanting to turn around and leave just as he'd done at the restaurant. He could never be in Juli's league. Her family had to be wealthy with a Spanish-style villa with its tile roof and beige stucco. He studied the arched veranda and the wide outside staircase leading to the second floor. Juli's apartment, he guessed.

He couldn't run away. Instead he tried to face the truth. Juli hadn't missed going to college because of funds. She'd followed her father's wishes and worked in his store. Store? Garlic Garden had to be a massive business. Knowing he couldn't sit there all night, Alan grasped his good sense and pulled into the driveway.

When he turned off the motor and stepped out of the car, Juli's voice greeted him. "I'm up here," she said, waving from the second level. He took the steps to the top, facing her bright smile, but behind it he saw worry.

"Come in," she said, motioning him through the door.

He stopped his mouth from gaping when he entered. Decorated in Southwest style, the room burst into sunset colors taken from a large painting hanging above the arched fireplace. "This is awesome, Juli. I can see why you don't want to move."

"But I must. I realize that more and more."

Her tentative comment caused him to ask, "Why?"

"I told you on Monday. I need to stand on my own and get out from under my parents' guidance. I'm twenty-five. Don't you think it's time?"

How could he answer that question? He bit the corner of his lip, wishing she hadn't asked. "I think it depends on the person. I couldn't answer for you."

She nodded. "I know, and it's my answer to the situation. Thanks so much for listening to me at the beach. It was so helpful. I felt you understood."

"I do. As much as a person can who doesn't know the whole situation."

"Today you will." Her face brightened. "Let's enjoy the day. Would you like to look around?"

He did, and he didn't. "Show me the way," he said, noticing the lavishness of the decor. The more he saw, the more ashamed he was of his small condo. He'd cut corners, even with his good salary, to help his mother.

She led him into her kitchen, where he noticed she hadn't begun to prepare dinner; then he glanced through the doorway of the other rooms, admiring a private balcony where she could read or sun herself. "It's a wonderful place, Juli. I'm sure it will be difficult to leave."

"It will in some ways."

He watched her expression change and wondered what was coming next.

"By the way, my mom insisted I invite you to dinner in their house. I tried to say no, but my mom is very persuasive."

His chest tightened. "You mean have dinner with your parents?"

"If you don't mind. It would make my mom happy."

Juli had mentioned meeting her parents but not eating dinner with them. He'd already been startled by their wealth, and now he'd have to make conversation. Then he was bowled over by another issue. He'd never told Juli he was a physician. It didn't seem right telling her in front of her parents.

"Mom promised she would go light on the garlic, but if that's a problem, we won't go."

He started to say it would be a problem, but he saw the look on her face and realized what he had to do. "Will it make you happy?"

"When Mom's happy, I am."

Her comment gave Alan great insight. She hadn't learned to say no. He knew Juli's faith was strong, and he wondered if the commandment about honoring parents had kept her tied to them so tightly. Maybe she thought following their every wish was honoring them, but *honor* had a deeper meaning to him. "I'll be careful with the garlic. It'll be fine."

"Thanks. I wanted you to meet them anyway."

Her face filled with relief while he managed to cover his hesitation. Juli telephoned her mother, and she said they would come then hung up and returned to his side. "They're ready with hors d'oeuvres."

Alan hoped he was.

He followed Juli down the staircase and along the veranda to the front door. Inside, the opulent space almost knocked him over. A grand foyer with a large open staircase greeted him when they entered. A tile floor led in a multitude of directions. Alan noticed a dining room to his right with the table set for four places. To his left he glimpsed a sizable living room, and ahead he could see a massive fireplace and assumed it was the family room.

Juli guided him in that direction, and the scent of herbs and beef met him as they neared the kitchen.

"Mom." Juli halted in the doorway. "This is Alan Louden." She turned to Alan. "My mother, Grace Maretti."

"Mrs. Maretti, your home is beautiful," Alan said, extending his hand.

She wiped her hands on a towel and greeted him. "We're so happy you're joining us." She motioned toward the large window facing the backyard. "Your dad's outside with the appetizers, Juli. You know how pleased he is with the patio. I'll give a call when dinner's on the table."

One down, Alan thought as he followed Juli into the backyard, again overwhelmed by the view and the size of the house grounds.

Juli's father rose from his chair and crossed the flagstone with long strides. "Alan, how nice to meet you."

"Same here, Mr. Maretti," he said, noticing a spread of fresh vegetables and chips with bowls of dip nearby.

"Would you care for some lemonade?" He gestured to the large pitcher. "Or Grace has some iced tea inside if you prefer."

"Lemonade is fine," he said, following Juli to the table for a glass. He put a few vegetables on the plate but skipped the dip, fearing it contained garlic.

Once he was settled, he addressed Juli's father. "Juli tells me you have a produce shop."

He sensed Juli's discomfort, and now he wished he'd told her he'd seen her at the farmers' market in Monterey.

"We focus on garlic along with gourmet products and a gift shop. Would you believe last year we had over 140,000 visitors?"

Alan drew back, not able to imagine that many people wanting to purchase garlic. "That's amazing."

"We own a large garlic farm, as well." His face filled with pride.

Confusion settled over Alan as he wondered what troubled Juli about her father's business. He owned a huge farm and an amazing store and had gained wealth from garlic. Alan bit into a celery stick.

Juli gave him a furtive look then turned away.

"I'm impressed," Alan said, hoping to waylay some of Juli's concerns. "Juli didn't let me know how extensive your business is."

"My little girl's modest."

Juli gave an exasperated huff. "Dad, I'm not a little girl anymore."

Her father just grinned. "To me you always will be."

She gave Alan a desperate look. "I know," she mumbled.

Alan saw the tension in her face. He was certain her parents were good people, but they had a firm grip on Juli. Until she let herself do what her heart desired, she would never be free.

"Our son helps run the business. He's got the business sense—went to college and all that."

"I've heard," Alan said. "Juli mentioned she didn't attend school so she could help you in the store."

"I did all of this without college myself. God gave me good old common sense, and I inherited some land from my father then added a few hundred acres later. Amazing what a person can do with the Lord's help." He sent a loving smile to Juli. "She's a great manager. We'd be lost without her at the store."

Alan watched the comment knife through the air and stab Juli in the heart. "You'd manage. She's trained everyone well, I'm sure."

"Dinner." Juli's mother's voice cut through his comment, saving them from further discussion. Alan sensed Juli was uneasy about what had just happened, and he hoped he hadn't added to her stress.

When they gathered around the dining room table, Juli's father offered a blessing, and the food was passed. The salad came first, followed by a pasta dish with a green sauce that made Alan pause. Had this been the pasta that had made him ill?

Mrs. Maretti must have noticed his questioning look. "I hope you like pesto. It's made with olive oil, basil, and pine nuts, mainly."

She hadn't mentioned the garlic, but he thought he caught a faint scent of it. "I'm not sure I've had it," he said, spooning a little on his plate. Next came a bowl of mixed vegetables and large hunks of homemade bread. He took a forkful of the pasta and enjoyed the delicious flavor. If it had garlic, it wasn't overpowering. Alan was thankful for that. While they ate, Juli's father talked about garlic. Alan learned about types of garlic, including California early and California late, the most common. Mr. Maretti detailed the planting and growing of garlic and explained how to break the bulbs into cloves. Alan had become an authority over a twenty-minute meal.

Mr. Maretti used his fork to make a gesture. "Did you know garlic is a bulb of the lily family?"

"No. Really?"

"It's also related to the chive and onion, but now that doesn't surprise you. Some garlic is flowering and edible."

Alan began to panic. He didn't know if it was too much information or if he was becoming ill. He felt a tingling sensation along his limbs, and he began to itch.

Mr. Maretti's voice faded in and out. "Did Juli tell you she was the Gilroy High Garlic Queen the year she graduated? It was—"

"Dad. Please." Juli's voice split the air. "That's enough about garlic."

She looked at Alan, and her eyes widened.

Alan gasped for breath.

"Are you okay?"

Juli bounded from her chair and darted to him. "Alan, you're sick." She turned to her father. "He can't breathe. Please call 911."

nine

Juli paced in the emergency waiting room while her father sat in a chair reading a magazine, but she witnessed tension in his face. At the house the EMT gave Alan a shot of epinephrine before taking him to the ambulance. Garlic. It had to be. Before she and her father left, her mother had been distraught, promising she'd put very little garlic in the pesto sauce.

"I added oil, pine nuts, basil, and just a pinch of garlic," she'd said.

Juli's frustration had reached its peak. "Our whole lives revolve around the rotten stuff."

"Juliana!" she'd snapped. "It's garlic that gave you this good life. I don't want to hear you talk like that."

"I'm sorry, Mom. It's just that—" How could she have explained that she'd allowed garlic to cause her so much unhappiness?

Pushing away her thoughts, Juli drew in a lengthy breath and plopped back into the chair beside her father.

He lifted his head from the magazine. "Alan will be fine, Juli. I've never heard of anyone dying from garlic." He patted her hand and gave her a gentle-hearted smile.

She pressed her hand against his. "I know."

She hung her head and closed her eyes. Juli wanted someone to blame for her troubles, but she had to face the truth. She had caused most of her own undoing. She'd blamed her mother for the sauce even though she'd made an effort to adjust the ingredients. She'd blamed garlic for all the problems in her life, and now that she looked back, she'd probably caused her own lack of friendships, just as Dill had said.

When her confidence flagged, she'd apparently become all business, in some way putting up a wall to avoid being hurt. How many people had she rejected because of the barricade she'd set up for herself?

College had been the same story. She'd wanted to go so badly but blamed her parents for not encouraging her. She'd put her dreams on hold for them, but was it really a fear of failure? *Lord, am I missing opportunities because of fear? If so, I haven't trusted You. Help me to see clearly.*

"Is someone waiting for Alan Louden?"

Juli spun around. "Yes." She rushed to the waiting room doorway and stepped into the hall with the doctor.

"Mr. Louden had dinner with you tonight."

"Yes. At my parents' house."

"He said he ate pasta. Could you give me more details?"

She explained about the meal, including the pasta dish. "Alan told me he had a problem with garlic."

"His reaction isn't from garlic."

"Not garlic?"

"That causes some stomach problems, and garlic dust can cause asthma symptoms, but Mr. Louden's problem was anaphylaxis."

"Anaphylaxis?"

"It's a severe and potentially fatal allergic reaction."

Juli felt breathless as her pulse accelerated. "Fatal?"

He nodded. "I'm afraid so. If he hadn't gotten here when he did, there would have been no guarantee. But don't worry—he's doing fine. He's been treated with corticosteroids, and he'll be able to go home, but he needs to carry an EpiPen with him. Certain nuts can cause this kind of allergic reaction, not garlic."

"Alan ate pesto sauce. It has pine nuts."

"Pine nuts. Now I understand. I'll talk with him about that."

Her shock gave way to relief. "Thank you, Doctor."

"You can see him in a few minutes. I'll send a nurse down."

"We'll be here. Thank you."

He walked away, and Juli stood there reeling with the news. Fatal. And more likely pine nuts than garlic. She turned and stepped back inside the waiting room.

"It's not the garlic," she told her dad. She sat beside him, and her tears broke through as she explained the news to her father. He wrapped his arm around her shoulder and let her weep against his chest. When she gained control, she sat up and wiped her eyes. "Sorry, Dad, but it was such a shock to hear the doctor say *fatal*."

"You don't have to apologize. I'm shocked, too." He patted her hand. "You really like this fellow, don't you?"

She saw something new in her father's eyes, tenderness she'd never noticed before. Swallowing her emotions, she nodded. "I do, but I don't want to rush anything, and I don't want to get hurt."

"Put it in the Lord's hands, honey. Listen to God in your heart, and you'll do okay."

She leaned her head against his shoulder. "Thanks, Daddy."

Juli sat there, resting against her father's chest and feeling safe and loved. Sadness washed over her as she thought how often she'd felt angry with him for his control when she'd been as much to blame for not expressing her desires and dreams to her parents.

"Juli Maretti."

The nurse's voice startled her. She pulled away from her dad and rose. "I'll be back in a few minutes," she said, hurrying toward the nurse.

"Don't rush," her dad said. "I'll call your mom. I know she's sitting by the phone."

The nurse's shoes scuffed along the corridor as Juli followed. The woman punched a button, and the emergency room doors opened. Juli stayed close behind her. White curtains divided the room into spaces, and they passed three before the woman stopped and pulled back the drape.

Juli stepped inside, and when she saw Alan, tears pooled in her eyes. "How are you feeling?" she asked, trying to control the quake in her voice.

"Much better now. I'm so sorry for this, and I'm totally embarrassed. Your parents must think I'm an oddball."

"No, they don't. They're concerned. Daddy's in the waiting room, calling Mom. I know she's worried." She rested her hand on his arm. "The doctor said you can go home."

"Good. I have medication, and I'll be fine now, but it came on so quickly I couldn't talk. I felt as if my throat had closed, and I couldn't breathe. I've never experienced that before."

She sat on the edge of the chair beside his bed. "And don't do it again, okay?"

Alan grinned. "I'll vote for that." His eyes searched hers. "It wasn't garlic, you know."

Her chest tightened at his smile. "I heard. He suspects pine nuts were the culprit." She brushed a strand of hair from his forehead.

"I've eaten nuts all my life. I assumed the problem was garlic. Not fair to judge without having all the facts."

"We do that all the time, don't we?"

He nodded as if understanding she meant far more than judging food.

The curtain shifted, and the doctor she'd met stepped into the cubicle. "You look much better. How are you feeling now?"

"Almost like new."

"You'll need to make an appointment with an allergist and go through the testing, but my guess is pine nuts. They come from a family that's different from most nuts, so often people don't realize they have an allergic reaction until times like this. It's good your girlfriend was on her toes."

Juli opened her mouth then closed it when Alan gave her a wink.

He tore a sheet from his prescription pad. "Here's the name

of an allergist in Monterey you can call, unless you have someone else in mind."

Alan glanced at the paper and grinned. "I know him. He works with me at Community Hospital."

"I'll send him your records."

"Thanks."

The doctor slipped the prescription pad into his pocket. "I suppose you'd like to get out of here."

Alan smiled. "I can't wait."

The doctor grinned at Juli. "I think I can leave you in the hands of this lovely young woman if you'd like to go."

Juli felt the same old heat rise on her neck. *Lovely young woman.* One day she hoped she could accept a compliment without blushing.

❧

Alan leaned against the chaise lounge on Juli's balcony and licked the fork. "This cake was delicious." He set the plate on a table beside him. "We should have stayed down with your mom and dad. They're probably disappointed."

"They understand. They're both happy you're okay."

Alan brushed strands of hair from his forehead. "I'm mortified that I scared them like that. I'll make an appointment with the allergist tomorrow, but until I learn differently, I know not to eat pine nuts."

"You'll have to be careful and check ingredients on any food that might have them."

"I will." His gaze drifted to the hilly landscape beyond the house. The sun had sunk below the mountain, and now the expanse of green trees had darkened to blue and the landscape lay in shadows. The sky had colored like an artist's palette of Southwest colors—orange, coral, and deep purple, reminding him of Juli's living room.

He watched Juli gazing at the sky. "The view is gorgeous. You'll miss that if you move away."

Her shoulders lifted in a sigh. "I know, but I'll never be who

I want to be if I don't. You've met my parents, and you can see they are strong people."

"But strong in a good way. They've stuck together and made a wonderful life for you. I admire that."

She nodded. "I know, and that's why it makes leaving difficult. I'm not sure they'll understand."

A question niggled his thoughts, and this seemed as good a time as any to ask. "Juli, why are you so uptight about your father's business? It's more than wanting to be a social worker."

Her head shot up as if she'd been stung by a bee. "What do you mean?"

"You told me your father sold produce. You said he had a store. You never told me he had garlic farms and a huge shop that made him a wealthy man. I was bowled over when I pulled up to the house today. I almost wanted to leave."

"Leave? Why?"

"I'm not wealthy, for one thing."

"Neither am I, Alan. My parents are."

"But mine never were. I grew up in a whole different world from yours, Juli. I'm rattled by the assumption I made, thinking you were trying to hide your poverty from me, a poverty I knew so well as a kid. I'm hurt that—"

"I'm sorry, but poverty or wealth makes no difference to me. I like you for who you are and not for how much money you have."

He straightened his back. "I'm happy to hear that, but along with everything else, you've been evasive. I pictured your family working in a little store that sold produce. Your life seemed on the same level as mine. You—"

"I'm going to move, Alan, and then I'll be really poor the way you want me."

He gave her a placating grin. "I don't want you poor, but I thought you were. Anyway, you'll never be poor. Your father—"

She drew back as if he'd slapped her. "I know it seems I've

lived off my father, but I pay rent and work hard. I'm finally getting the gumption to make changes, and all I can do is hope the Lord will bless me."

Silence hung on the air except for the buzzing of cicadas filling the night sky.

"You're right." He leaned forward and folded his hands on his knees. "You're being positive, and I'm dragging along my old memories instead of accepting my blessings."

She didn't respond for a moment. "Me, too, Alan. We're all lugging the old baggage around." She tilted back her head and rubbed her neck then released a lengthy sigh. "Maybe I should try to explain what's bothered me for so long."

He swung his legs over the edge of the chaise lounge and motioned her to his side. She rose, and they sat together facing the foothills and the first stars of evening.

"I wasn't popular in high school. I had bookish friends. The popular kids called us nerds."

Disbelieving, he shifted his gaze to her dark curling hair and her lovely mouth that so often curved to a smile for him. "You're kidding."

"I wouldn't kid about something like that. When the popular kids gave parties, I wasn't invited. It hurt me."

"Did you ever think they were envious?"

Her hand flew to her chest. "Envious of me? Now you're kidding."

He grasped her shoulders and turned her to face him. "I can't believe you don't know how amazing you are. You're beautiful, Juli. Inside and out." His eyes swept over her frame, her slender body, the slope of her delicate shoulders, her graceful neck covered by the dark curling waves.

She didn't speak, and her eyes searched his as if she were waiting for his admission of a cruel joke.

Alan opened his heart. "I'm startled you really don't know this."

"My family never looked for outward beauty. We grew up

to be grateful for God's goodness to us. My dad worked hard. He was a wonderful employer and had good workers who returned every harvest. I never judged people that way."

He slipped his arm around her shoulders. "But others do. People try to undercut things that are a threat to them."

"I've never been a threat. Many of those kids' families had money. Maybe it was my personality. I was quiet. I know you don't see that now, but I was. I didn't have a lot of confidence. I didn't dress the way they did. I was different, so how could I be a threat?"

"Your goodness is a threat because it makes you stand out. People can ignore those who aren't a threat, those who aren't in their way to success, but they plot a course to wipe out competition. You must have been an amazing threat to those people. Were they all as wealthy as your family?"

"Wealthy? You mean with money, right?"

He nodded, astounded at her philosophy, a wonderful one he had to admit, and it made him care about her even more.

"No. Many of them lived in smaller houses, but I never flaunted my home."

"You didn't have to. They saw it and your life as better than theirs, and they couldn't handle it."

She shook her head. "I can't believe that."

"You can't understand it. That's all." His mind shifted back to earlier in the evening. "Your dad started to tell me something about your being the Gilroy High Garlic Queen. What's that all about?"

"That was the worst."

"What do you mean 'the worst'? Wasn't that an honor?"

"Yes, it was a big honor because the Gilroy High Garlic Queen also participated in the garlic festival each year in July."

"Did they pick someone or—"

Her eyes widened. "No, it was a vote. The whole school voted."

"And you won." His mind spun with confusion. The whole

school voted, and she won. He couldn't understand her problem.

"It turned out to be a plot to embarrass me."

"A plot? The whole school was in on a plot?"

She lowered her eyes, and he waited while she pondered what he'd asked. When she lifted her head, he saw confusion in her eyes. "That's what I thought when it happened."

"You assumed that those who taunted you controlled the vote."

"They were popular and usually did."

Alan tilted her chin upward to look in her eyes. "Apparently not this time. The underclassmen voted for the person they liked and thought was worthy of the title."

She nodded. "I learned the truth later. The underclassmen were tired of the snobbishness and decided to vote for me, but the others—the popular kids—decided to make sure I won."

"Why?"

"The king always presented the queen with a bouquet of roses, but that year it wasn't roses."

"Okay." He hung on her every word and waited.

"It was roses and garlic bulbs."

"Garlic bulbs." He chuckled. "You mean the things that look like onions?"

Her face filled with mortification.

"That's inventive. Why didn't you laugh?"

"How could I? I was horrified."

"Why? *They* gave you the flowers, dear Juli. If anyone was at fault, it was the person who gave you the flowers."

"He and a couple of others were suspended and missed the graduation ceremony, but meanwhile I could never let it go." Her eyes widened. "The other day a girl I knew in high school came into the store with a college sorority friend. Guess how she introduced me."

"The Gilroy High Garlic Queen?"

She closed her eyes and shook her head. "The one who

received the garlic and rose bouquet."

Alan drew her into his arms. "I love it. What could be more perfect for a garlic queen than a rose and garlic bouquet?"

Her eyes widened as if discovering a truth. "You love it now that you know."

In a moment she began to laugh, and Alan drew her closer, enjoying every moment.

When they'd quieted, he brushed her cheek with his hand. "We've known each other for nearly a month."

"We have. It's been so nice, and thank you for the good laugh. I need to learn to do that more when it comes to things that really hurt."

"Laughter is the best medicine."

"Proverbs says a cheerful heart is good medicine."

"You see, even the Bible agrees." He felt his mouth next to hers. " Juli."

She lowered her gaze, and he felt her release a faint shudder. Without asking, he lowered his lips to hers. Her mouth felt soft and warm. When he drew back, her eyes stayed riveted to his mouth, and he lowered his lips again and kissed hers lightly.

They sat in the quiet of the evening with the cicadas' song as their music, but nothing filled his heart more than holding Juli in his arms.

ten

Juli closed her cell phone and slipped from her car then hit the remote. As she headed toward the soup kitchen, she noticed Alan's car already parked in the lot. Her heart skipped, and she grinned, recalling his caring ways. He'd opened so many doors for her and helped her admit what she longed for so often.

The stuffy kitchen pressed against her as she stopped at the list to check her station then headed toward the salad bar, grateful she didn't have to cook.

Alan waved, and she waved back then noticed Tom had come again. He looked at her with expectation.

"She's not feeling well," she mouthed.

Tom shrugged and came closer.

"Megan just called," she said. "She's feeling ill. It's the sunburn. She said you went to the beach."

"I told her to use lotion," he said, rolling his eyes. "I'll check on her later." He walked away and settled in beside Angie.

Seeing the two together gave Juli a start. Angie seemed to gravitate toward the unattached males, and Tom appeared to be enjoying the attention.

Alan stepped beside her and rested his hand on her shoulder. "What's up?" He tilted his head toward Tom.

"He asked about Megan. She's too sunburned to come."

"Too bad," he said, but he seemed to linger.

Finally she turned toward him. "Is something wrong?"

His face validated what she sensed, and she looked over his shoulder.

"Tom?"

He nodded.

114

"I've warned Megan."

He drew in a breath. "Tom's looking for fun. If Megan's getting too serious, I think she'll scare him away."

As they spoke, Juli could see Tom using the same come-ons he used with Megan. He whispered in Angie's ear, and she touched her chin to her shoulder with a giggle then shooed him back to his job.

"We've done all we can," Juli said, wishing Megan had listened, but Tom's behavior upset her anyway.

"Talk later," Alan said and headed back to his station.

Juli pulled the packages of lettuce from the double refrigerator, removed the cellophane, rinsed the leaves, and began to chop the greens. She wanted to throttle Tom then asked the Lord for forgiveness. She expected he would eventually break Megan's heart. Friendship was precious, and she again thanked the Lord for someone in her life like Alan.

Megan had become too involved with Tom. She'd said it to her face, and though Megan claimed to be a believer, she'd missed the mark with her behavior. Juli cringed. She'd done the same but in a different way. She'd lacked trust in both the Lord and Alan, but she was working on it and prayed she could truly place her confidence in God and rely on Alan.

Her gaze drifted back to Tom, and she turned away, disgusted at his behavior. While she worked on the salad, she noticed they were shorthanded tonight. As much as Tom upset her, his being there helped them get the food ready for the people waiting outside. She could credit him for that. She hurried to finish her job, and it wasn't long before Bill gave the signal he was opening the doors. Everyone moved as fast as they could to bring the food trays into the dining room. Alan stepped beside her with the rolls and butter, and he and Juli doled out the portions.

After serving, Juli took time to speak to those who looked lonely or needed a listening ear, and she noticed Alan kneeling beside a woman who'd been sitting with her head braced on her hand. The earnest look on his face touched her. She'd been pleased to see he'd become more confident in speaking to the people, and she witnessed real concern on his face.

When people began to leave, Juli looked at the wall clock. They could be out of there by 9:00 if they hurried. Alan had said they would talk later, and she'd set her heart on it. As she neared him, she noticed him holding a younger man's hand, and she suspected he was taking his pulse. She thought of something her father had often said: "You can take the boy out of the country, but you can't take the country out of the boy." It reminded her of Alan. He could leave the hospital for the evening, but he seemed to bring his nursing skills with him. Maybe that's what loving a career meant.

She carried trays into the kitchen and pulled out the cloths and bucket, poured in the disinfectant, added water, and returned to the dining room to clean the tables. This time she saw Alan sitting beside an elderly woman, her hand in his. She paused a moment, struck by what she'd missed earlier. Alan's head was bowed, and her heart melted as she saw him in prayer with the woman.

The next time she looked, Alan was nowhere to be seen. She hurried into the kitchen and found Alan standing beside the commercial dishwasher, moving a receptacle of trays into the machine.

"How did you get stuck here?" she asked after putting away the bucket and cloths.

"I might as well help while I wait for you."

"Looks like I'm finished."

He pulled off the plastic gloves and wrapped his arm around her shoulder. "I have something I want to show you. Want to go for a ride?"

"A ride?"

"Just for a while. It's warm, and I thought we could zoom down to the beach and take a walk."

The thought of a cool breeze excited her, and though Juli disliked the ride home after dark, spending time with Alan made it worthwhile. "Okay. I can't pass up a beach walk."

They said good night to Bill while he packed the last of the supplies away; then they headed outside. Even there the fresh air felt wonderful. She settled into Alan's car, and he walked around to the driver's side and slid in.

"Here's an offer for you," she said, grasping the opportunity.

"That sounds interesting."

"Have you ever been to the Gilroy Garlic Festival? I know how much you love garlic."

He chuckled. "I think you have your facts wrong, but no, I've never had the pleasure. Tell me about it."

"It's a fund-raiser that supports charitable groups and service organizations in Gilroy. I'm expected to be there, but it's not just garlic products. They have music and crafts. Dad has a booth in the vendors' section and donates his profits to the cause. It's a nice event."

"And you were the queen of garlic."

She waved his comment away. "Forget that. I try to."

"Never forget, Juli. People chose you to be the queen. It was an honor, and it will be an honor for me to go with you."

"Thanks. I wanted you to see the good side of garlic."

"I know one good side. You."

She gave him a poke. "I suppose I should say thanks."

He slid the key into the ignition, but before pulling away, he leaned around his headrest into the backseat.

"Here," he said, handing her a pile of brochures.

Looking at the one on top sent Juli's heart on a wild ride. "Where did you get these?"

"I stopped by the university and picked them up for you."

She gazed at the brochures, touched by his thoughtfulness. "That was so sweet of you."

"Not as sweet as you are." He started the engine and headed out to the highway.

Juli grinned then opened the first pamphlet and studied the information. "What's this Collaborative Health and Human Services curriculum?"

"It looked like what you need for social work. It gives you all the essential skills and training needed in the health and social service area. A bachelor's degree in that prepares you for a master's program in public health or social work." He pointed to the information. "I read a couple of them. They explain a lot of things, and from what I can tell, you can work in a related field while getting your master's."

She chuckled. "You know lots more than I do about this."

"You'll know it, too, once you read the material. I'm excited for you."

"So am I." She ran her hand over the shiny pamphlets. Holding them in her hands made her decision seem more real than she imagined; yet it also added to her difficulty. "I have to talk with Mom and Dad. I know it's going to shock them."

"It'll grow on them, Juli. When you look over the pamphlets, you'll see that some of the classes are offered online, or part of the class is that way. It will help when you're still working at the store."

"Online. I hadn't thought about that possibility." She shuffled through the brochures, noting the information each covered as Alan slowed and pulled into the beach parking area.

He found a spot, turned off the engine, and opened the door. "I checked Gavilan and Harnell College on the Internet, but they don't seem to have a social work curriculum. I know they're closer to you than Monterey."

"You did all that for me?"

He winked at her, closed the door, and came around to the passenger side. He held the door while she climbed out, and when she rose, they stood nose to nose. "I'll climb a mountain for you, Juli."

His lips were so close to hers, and her heart skipped as she felt herself stretching to kiss him. Her lips touched his as he drew her closer in an embrace that made her giddy.

"I've never kissed anyone before," she said as she tilted back to look into his eyes.

He gave her a questioning look. "That can't be true. We kissed the other night. You haven't forgotten already?"

She looked into his moonlit eyes. "I'd never forget that. I mean I've never initiated a kiss before. I can't believe I did that."

"Believe it, and don't stop. I loved every second. You're amazing."

She gestured toward the brochures on the seat. "So are you."

He wove his fingers through hers as they ambled to the sand. They slipped off their shoes and walked barefoot toward the water. Juli stepped in first, the white foam rolling forward. She felt the wave recede, pulling the earth back into the bay from beneath her feet. Alan rolled up his pant legs and joined her. They laughed when a wave splashed higher than the others and dampened their clothes. Then, throwing caution aside, she ran along the surf with Alan as the wind blew through her hair and a cooler breeze swept across her arms.

When they tired of the run, they returned to the sand, their feet sinking into the crystals while Alan enfolded her shoulders with his arm.

She nestled against his side. "You always think of the most wonderful things to do."

He chuckled. "A walk on the beach is wonderful?"

"I've never had this kind of relationship."

He arched his eyebrow.

"Really."

He arched both eyebrows.

"Never. Honest. You're such a special friend."

"You're special, too, Juli, and never forget it."

Alan became quiet. He shifted his gaze ahead of him as

if in thought. "You've been so blessed, Juli, and yet you're so down to earth. So humble."

"I'm who I am. It's my parents' money, not mine."

He turned and faced her. "But you had luxuries and benefits a lot of kids don't have." He closed his eyes, and when he opened them, they were filled with sadness. "Kids like me."

"Kids like you? You went to college. I didn't."

"But that was hard work and blessings. I told you my dad died and my mom raised all five of us, but it wasn't easy."

The serious look she saw concerned her. "What is it, Alan?"

He shook his head. "Remembering."

She moved closer and twined her fingers through his. "You can tell me."

"It's hard to talk about it, Juli. Really difficult."

"I told you about my teen years. That was hard for me to talk about."

"I know it was, and I'm glad you did, but this is different."

Juli's mind spun with possibilities. She wanted to know everything about him, but she wanted to respect his privacy. "Never mind," she said, seeing the distress on his face. "Some other time." She moved ahead of him.

He followed her back to the car, both of them in silence. Alan opened the passenger door, and she slipped in. He rounded the car and settled beside her. When the engine kicked in, Alan pulled from the parking lot onto the highway.

The situation had put a strain on their conversation, and Juli slumped against the seat while another problem dropped into her thoughts, a problem she'd meant to discuss with him. Tom and Angie.

Since she'd watched Tom with Angie, Juli wondered what she should say to Megan. Nothing would be best, but how could she witness Tom's behavior and not say anything? She needed to pray about it. Juli looked at Alan out of the corner of her eye. "What should we do about Tom and Angie?"

She'd pulled him from his thoughts, she guessed, because

he gave her a blank look before he seemed to understand. He shook his head. "Best to stay out of it, I suppose."

"But it's so difficult. I should avoid spending time with Megan, I think, because that's the safest. I'm so afraid to say something yet afraid of not saying anything. When Megan starts mooning over Tom again, I don't know how I can keep quiet."

Alan kept his eyes focused on the traffic. "It's difficult, but I'm not sure either of us can do any good. We've both tried."

She nodded, recalling the edgy conversations she and Megan had already had and how little good they did. Megan would have to learn the hard way, but it saddened her.

"Tom was open with me about his attitude." He glanced her way. "Marriage isn't in his future. If Megan assumed it was, she'll have to deal with it. I know that sounds cruel, but your getting involved can destroy your friendship with her, and when things end between Megan and Tom, she'll need a friend."

His words spread over her like a balm. "You're right. She'll really need a good friend."

She looked out the passenger window into the night sky. "I'll have to keep quiet, but that's going to take a lot of effort."

They fell into silence again, and soon Alan pulled into the soup kitchen lot beside Juli's car. He turned toward her. "Juli, I'm sorry about tonight. I've been plagued by my past, and I've allowed it to affect who I am today."

"I'm fine now. I understand. I did the same thing with my hang-up about Gilroy and everything related to it."

He reached for her hand and wove his fingers between hers. "The reason the soup kitchen means so much to me is because that's where we ate many of our meals. Not this soup kitchen, but others."

A wave of sadness washed over her. "You did?"

"My mom struggled to feed us after my dad died. The little insurance he had barely buried him, and his illness had eaten up most of their savings. Mom did the best she could, but when we were desperate, she marched us into a soup kitchen. It was usually the only real meal we had that day."

Juli felt tears pool in her eyes. "Alan, you could have told me. I understand."

"You understand with sympathy and pity, but no one can understand unless they've lived in that situation. I dealt with it, but watching my mom's shame and seeing her deprecated is something I still can't bear."

His words were disconcerting. She had never known poverty, and he was right. She could never really understand. "I don't know what to say."

"Say anything but you're sorry. I don't want pity, Juli. I'm proud we got through the bad times. I'm thrilled I did well in school and got scholarships and government aid because of our poverty status. God's been good to us, and now I can help my mom."

Juli shifted and put her hand on his face. "You're a good person, Alan. I won't say I'm sorry. I'm grateful you've been blessed."

She leaned back and spotted the car clock. "It's really late. I need to get going."

Alan grasped her arm. "One more minute? While I'm talking, Juli, I might as well clear the air completely. I've wanted to tell you something else. It'll sound dumb, but I hope you understand why—"

A loud *thump* sounded as something hit the car window, causing both of them to jump.

Juli saw a man's face peering in the window. "Who is that?"

"A drunk." Alan shook his head. "He probably wants money. I'll give him a couple of bucks, but he looks in bad shape—so when I step out, I want you to open your door and get into your car. I don't want any trouble. He might be on drugs. Are you listening?"

"I can't leave you."

"Yes, you can. I want you to get in your car and lock the door then get out of here."

The man tugged on the door handle then pounded against the window again until Juli feared it would break.

She riveted herself to the seat. "I won't."

"You will."

The determination in his voice forced her to give in. Alan wouldn't move until she left, and she feared the man would break his window or get more violent.

"Be careful," she said, pushing her remote then flinging open the door and bounding into her car. Her fingers trembling, she slammed the door shut and slipped the key into the ignition. Outside, she heard the man cursing and Alan's softer voice mingling with his.

She backed up and pulled down the driveway, but instead of leaving, she watched through her side mirror until the man spotted her and started running toward her. She shifted into drive and tore out of the parking lot, praying Alan would be safe.

eleven

Alan watched the man veer toward Juli's car. The man's stagger delayed his steps while Alan prayed she would get out of there fast. When she sped away, he jumped into his car and peeled out toward the parking lot exit with the man chasing him. The man's muddled thinking saved Alan. No reasoning would have delayed the thief from using the knife he'd pulled from his pocket to take Alan's wallet. He wasn't happy with the couple of bills he'd tried to give him.

Alan wanted to wring Juli's neck for not leaving immediately. He understood why. She was worried about his well-being, but her delay could have caused both of them problems. He wouldn't let that happen again. "Thank You, Lord," he said aloud, grateful for God's protection. He shook his head, trying to clear his thoughts.

Alan pulled out his cell phone and hit Juli's number. Instead of getting the usual voice mail, he listened as her phone rang. When he heard her voice, he relaxed. "I'm fine," he said. "Are you okay?"

"Scared, but fine. What happened?"

He told her about everything but the knife.

"I'm sorry I didn't leave as you told me, but I wanted to make sure you were okay."

"We're both fine now, but let's not do that again. We should have learned our lesson from the purse-snatching incident. I'm sorry—I wasn't thinking."

He heard her deep sigh. "And ruin the most excitement I've ever had in my life."

He chuckled but managed to remain firm. "I mean it, Juli."

"I know you do."

Her contrite voice touched him. "Call me when you get home. Please. I want to know you're safe."

"I will. Promise."

He closed the lid of his cell phone and slipped it into his shirt pocket. Weariness rolled over him, some due to the adrenaline rush he'd had from the addict who wanted his money and some due to frustration.

Tonight he'd planned to be open with Juli. He'd made such a secret out of his career, and now it had turned into a monster. Since he had opened the door to his difficult past, he thought the time seemed right to tell her about his work. He wanted to do it face-to-face and not over the phone. He didn't want to make a big deal out of it either. Driving to her house made the revelation too dramatic. He wanted it low key, but he had to work long hours this weekend, and seeing her soon seemed unlikely.

Alan wished Juli lived closer to Monterey. Gilroy was a lengthy drive to Monterey to see each other when they had conflicting work schedules, but even though that was the case, right now he wanted to advise her to stay in her apartment. Paying for school and cutting back on work meant less income. Living where she did made more sense

Conflicts. They seemed to be a part of life. Not everything went smoothly, especially when working on a solid relationship. Juli had made it clear that trust was important to her. Despite her own misgivings, she'd opened up about the things that troubled her, and she'd told him her dreams. He'd fallen short by not being open and honest with her. He'd never lied, but he'd left things unsaid.

Lacking openness and honesty seemed to be Tom's problem. He'd led Megan astray with his empty promises. The situation turned Alan's stomach. He believed respect was a major part of any relationship, especially a romantic relationship. Yet Tom had led Megan on, letting her think he had serious intentions when he had nothing but getting his way and then dropping her for a new opportunity.

Do not judge. The words washed over him. Maybe Tom had been open, and Megan had failed to heed his warning. Either way it was a rotten situation.

❧

When the telephone rang, Juli dropped the brochure and headed for the phone. Her hello was greeted by sobs.

"What happened, Megan?" Juli didn't have to ask. She could guess Tom had dumped her for Angie. In a few weeks Tom would dump Angie for some other woman eager for love, but what they found in Tom wasn't love. It was empty desire and nothing more.

"Tom dumped me," Megan finally mumbled between her tears.

"Megan, I don't know what to say." Good riddance was one thing, but Megan's feelings were what mattered now. "When I introduced you to Tom, I had no idea who he was. I thought he was Alan's friend, and Alan is such a good Christian."

"It's not your fault. You warned me, and I didn't listen." A hiccup sob cut through her words.

"Forget that now. That's not important. Do you want me to come over?"

"You're not busy?"

"I'm just sitting here. I'll get ready and be there in an hour or so." Juli looked at her watch, calculating Saturday's traffic.

"What about Alan?" Megan's question gave away her sadness.

"He's working a long shift this weekend. Everyone at the hospital seems to be taking vacations."

"Could you"—another sob broke into her sentence—"could you come?"

"Right away. See you soon."

Juli placed the receiver in the cradle and hurried to her bedroom. She took out a pair of capri pants and a top, pulled a comb through her tangled hair, and ran gloss over her lips.

Before she drove away from the house, Juli took a chance

and hit Alan's cell phone number. If he was busy, she knew he would ignore the call. When he answered, her heart soared. "I hate to bother you."

"What's wrong?"

The concern in his voice meant so much to her. "It's Megan. She called, and I'm heading over that way. She's so upset."

"I know. Tom told me this afternoon he ditched her. I wondered if she'd call you." His voice softened. "I should have warned you, but I didn't want to upset you."

"It's okay, but I honestly don't know what to say to her. I feel bad even though I know it was as much her fault as his."

"Be supportive and speak from your heart. That's all you can do."

"It seems like so little. They saw each other so often, too often, really, and—"

"I know. What can you say to someone whose trust has been shattered? I'm glad I'm not in your shoes."

"They're way too small for you," Juli said, struggling to be lighthearted. "I'd better go. It'll take me awhile to get there."

"Be careful driving home."

"Maybe I'll stay there overnight. Don't worry. I just wanted to hear your voice."

"I miss you, Juli. That's the bad thing about this job. The hours are crazy. You know I'll be sending up prayers for both of you."

"Thanks. That's what we need. I—I'll talk with you later." The words *I love you* had nearly slipped from her mouth. She closed her cell phone, wishing she could say those words aloud to Alan.

To her, those three words held a deep commitment. She felt certain she loved Alan, but making a lifetime commitment tied her in knots. They'd only met weeks ago, and how could she be sure this wasn't puppy love rather than the real thing? Megan's situation came to mind.

Still, confidence burned in her heart. Alan filled her image of a soul mate, a man who respected her, who wanted only the best for her and could trust her with the story of his difficult childhood, and a man she could trust. It had taken time for him to open up, but he had. She'd told him everything, and now that the doors were opening, each had shared their deepest hurts and worries. To Juli that was love.

Even more wonderful, he was a Christian, and she sensed that God had guided their steps to meet. She thought back to the day Bill had asked her to train Alan at the soup kitchen. They'd hit it off so well that day. They'd teased and yet talked about having a purpose in life to help others. It seemed perfect.

As Juli drove, she dug deep for any wisdom she might have tucked in the caverns of her mind. She searched in her heart for God's Word. Thinking of Megan feeling abandoned and used by someone who had such little feeling for her overwhelmed Juli. How could Megan be so blind?

Blind. What if she'd been in Megan's situation? What if Alan had been taking her for the same kind of ride? Would she have been wise enough to see the truth? The idea unsettled her. She clamped off the thought. Alan would never hurt her. Never.

The traffic thickened as Juli drew closer to Monterey. Instead of driving on the main tourist thoroughfare, she turned away from the bay toward the city, where traffic would be lighter. The closer she came to Megan's, the more uneasy she became. "Lord, give me words and wisdom." Her prayer rose, and she felt her shoulders lift.

When she reached Megan's building, she took time walking to her apartment. Every step that drew her closer made her feel less capable of being a source of help. Source of help? What made her think she would be Megan's source of help? A Bible verse entered her thoughts. *"My help comes from the LORD, the Maker of heaven and earth. He will not let your foot slip—he who watches over you will not slumber."* This was Megan's source of help. Juli recognized she was only the messenger.

❧

Alan leaned back in the cafeteria chair, thinking about Juli. He couldn't wait to see her. The past week they'd talked on the phone, but that was it. She worked during the day, and he'd been working the long night shift then sleeping during the day, exhausted from overtime in the ER. He'd even missed Wednesday at the soup kitchen. Though the volunteer job meant work, too, he loved it there. Another week of nights, and then he'd be scheduled back to his regular shift and have some days off. He couldn't wait.

This weekend he finally had a day off, and he planned to catch some sleep tomorrow morning and then go to the garlic festival with Juli. The idea made him chuckle. Alan Louden and the garlic festival—but he was falling in love with Juli, and garlic was an important part of her life. What he wouldn't do for love.

"What's so funny?"

Alan turned to face Tom. "Nothing's funny."

"You had a stupid look on your face."

"I was thinking about Juli and the garlic festival."

Tom snorted. "With your aversion to garlic, this sounds like love to me."

Although Tom was kidding, Alan wasn't. "I think you're right. She means more to me than I can tell you."

"Really?" He tucked his hands into the pockets of his lab coat. "Sorry I can't say the same."

Alan didn't want to deal with his romantic liaisons. "You already told me you broke up with Megan."

"Not Megan." He grasped a chair, pulled it to the end of the table beside Alan, and sat.

"No?"

"Angie."

"What do you mean?" Alan braced himself and wondered what was coming next.

"I really had fun with Megan, and she cared about me."

Alan had to bite his tongue from saying what was on his heart. "She did. She trusted you."

"I know. Now I realize how much I care about her. It's a new experience for me, Alan." He lowered his head. "I messed up. You got me thinking about being a Christian and about what God expects. I messed up double. Megan and God."

Alan's eyebrows raised. He'd never seen Tom look so serious. "What made the difference now?"

"I've thought about you and Juli. Your relationship is so strong. I've thought about what you said about respect, and I realize I haven't respected women much at all. Not even Megan." He lifted his head, discomfort on his face. "And I want to be honest with you. I didn't get that intimate with Megan. I tried, but she held me off. What I insinuated was just locker room talk. I should have respected her more."

Tom's confession startled Alan. He drew in a lengthy breath. "What do you want to do, Tom?"

"I want to make it right with Megan. What would you do, Alan?"

"I can't imagine being in that situation, so I'm not a good person to ask, but first you need to make it right with God. You need to open your heart to Him and spend some time in prayer, asking for His direction."

Tom closed his eyes and nodded. "I know. I've followed in my dad's footsteps, I think. He ran around on my mom, and they finally got divorced. It wasn't fun, Alan. It's not an excuse, but I guess I thought men were supposed to be like that. That's why I never thought about marriage. I guess I didn't want to ruin my own kids' lives with divorce, so it seemed impossible. But now. . .it's different."

Alan had never known about Tom's past, and he prayed the Holy Spirit would give Tom a double dose of God's direction and assurance.

"I know you're not an expert, but I'd still like to hear what you have to say."

Alan thought a moment. "You know I move more slowly than you. First I want to like and respect the woman I'm dating." He held up his hand. "And don't think I don't feel passion. I'm human, but passion doesn't last forever. Love does, and once trust is destroyed, it's difficult to regain. I guess my advice is move slowly. Prove yourself."

"I realize there's no guarantee with Megan. I don't know if she'll take me back, but I could try."

Alan shifted closer and rested his hand on Tom's shoulder. "This is when I turn to God for help. You've probably not been on speaking terms with the Lord very often, but it's never too late. Our imperfections allow God to show His power. 'My power is made perfect in weakness.' That's what He tells us. Think about it."

Tom looked thoughtful. "Thanks. I know you could blow me off and tell me I made my bed and can lie in it now, but you didn't. That means a lot to me." He shook Alan's hand then stood and walked away.

Alan let out a lengthy breath, amazed at Tom's revelation. He'd never seen Tom regret his actions, at least not like this, and to hear him say he needed God was awesome. He'd bounced from one woman to another. Each romance lasted until a new face came along and caught Tom's attention. He'd never showed a sign of remorse, and from Alan's memory he'd never longed to return to an old girlfriend. Something had happened to Tom.

❧

"Juli."

Her mother's voice floated down the hallway, and Juli came from the bedroom, adjusting the second outfit she'd tried on. "Hi," she said, surprised to see her mother. "I thought you'd left for the festival."

"Your dad's slow this morning, and he wanted to know where we should meet for dinner."

Juli held back a frown. "Meet for dinner? Alan's picking me

up. . .and I'm not sure if we're eating at the festival. You know how he is about garlic."

Her mother widened her eyes. "I thought his allergy was pine nuts."

"Yes, but—" How could she explain that some people weren't crazy about garlic? "He should be here any minute. I'll ask him."

"Good. Your dad wants to get to know him better."

Juli grinned. Not just her dad—her mom wanted to know Alan, too. She heard it in her voice, and she knew why. They realized Alan had become important in her life. "I'll give you a call when he gets here."

Her mother's gaze lowered to the lamp table beside Juli's recliner, and Juli's stomach rose to her throat. She watched her mother reach for the brochures she'd been perusing.

"What's this?" Her mother turned the pamphlets over then turned them back. She flipped through the stack then lifted her head. "What's this about?"

Juli drew up her shoulders. "I'm thinking about taking some classes."

"But these are health and human service classes. What does that have to do with business?"

Juli's chest tightened. Today of all days wasn't a time she wanted to get into this. She'd been praying and searching her heart for the best way to explain her longing to her parents. "It has nothing to do with business, Mom."

Her mother tossed them on the table. "Then I don't understand."

"It's something I would like to do for me."

Her mother's face filled with a quizzical look.

"Like nursing. You said you'd thought about being a nurse."

Her mother shook her head as if Juli were dense. "But I didn't become a nurse, did I? I became your mother. Your dad counts on you in the store, Juli. What would he do without you?"

She drew in a lengthy breath. "Alan answered that the other

day. I've trained people well, and we have trusted employees who've been with us, Mom. Dad would manage fine without me, but I'm not leaving the store tomorrow or next week." She released an exasperated sigh. "Please—I'm just looking at the brochures. Let's not get into this now. I'm not you. I don't have children to raise."

"But you will." She swung her hand toward the doorway. "Alan's been seeing you for some time now. He's a nice young man, and your dad and I have hopes. I realize he's not in the same financial situation we are, but he's young. Your father and I struggled at first, too, and look at us now."

" 'Store up for yourselves treasures in heaven. For where your treasure is, there your heart will be also.'" The scripture verse sailed from Juli's mouth before she could stop it.

Her mother's eyes widened, and Juli wanted to pull the verse back into her heart.

"My heart is with the Lord, Juliana. A person can be well off and still be a believer. I'm shocked at what you've insinuated."

Juli crossed to her mother's side and put her arms around her. "I wasn't insinuating anything. I was trying to make a point. For me, wealth isn't important, but being of service to others is. I've had the longing for years to help people, and lately I've thought about being a social worker, even a counselor. But I put it aside because I know how much Dad wants me at the store. You know how much I love volunteering at the soup kitchen, and I realize it's because that's what I want to do."

Her mother flung her arms upward. "If that's what you want, I can't stop you."

"I'm not going to abandon the store. I can go to school part-time."

"I suppose Alan gave you this idea."

Juli pulled away. "Alan has nothing to do with this, but he's listened, and he supports my idea. He's the one who told me classes are offered online so I could still work."

"At least he has a brain in his head."

Juli's arms went limp. "And I don't?" She wanted to ask why her brother had been encouraged to go to school and she hadn't been after she'd graduated, but that would only cause more dissension.

"I didn't mean that." Her mother sank into Juli's favorite chair. "It's just a shock, and you've never talked it over with us." She fingered the brochures then pushed them into a stack.

"I'd planned to discuss it with you and Dad once I decided what I'd like to do. I wanted to have a plan—find a way I could attend college and still work, at least part-time."

Her honesty had caused another notch in the argument. "Part-time?"

"Whatever. I'm still giving it thought." She crouched beside her mother. "Please don't run downstairs and start something with Dad today. Alan will be here any minute, and we're going to the festival. I promise I'll talk with him tomorrow if you think I should, but I really thought you'd both be more encouraging if I had solid plans in my mind."

Her mother drew in a lengthy breath and released a deep sigh. "I hate keeping things from your father."

"I know, Mom, but—"

The doorbell chimed, and Juli froze for a moment then closed her eyes and opened them again. "Please." She turned and headed to the door.

Alan's face glowed when his gaze met hers. "I've missed you so much."

She tried to give him a signal with a slight tilt of her head. "I've missed you, too." She opened the door wider, and when he stepped in, she saw the surprise on his face.

"Hello, Mrs. Maretti. It's good to see you again."

Her mother nodded and rose from the chair, looking as if she carried the weight of the world on her shoulders. "Thank you, Alan." She walked past him toward the door. "Call me when you decide where we should meet for dinner, Juliana." She hustled outside and shut the door.

Alan's befuddled look would have made Juli laugh if she were in a better mood.

"Juliana?"

Juli tried to push her doldrums aside. "That's my full name. Everyone calls me Juli unless they're upset."

"I guessed something was wrong."

Juli motioned toward the table. "She walked in and found those. I didn't know she was coming."

Alan eyed the brochures then looked back at her with a frown. "You mean you have to hide them from your family?"

"Unless I want a big commotion, like right now."

"You're not a child."

"Tell them, Alan." Tears blurred her eyes. "I love my parents to death. They're wonderful and so good to my brother, Jim, and me, but they get an idea in their heads—an idea they think is good for us—and they can't get it out. It's like a legacy, I guess. My dad created this huge business and expects us to love it as much as he does." The tears couldn't be contained, and she felt them flowing down her cheeks. "I hurt my mom's feelings today with scripture. Can you believe it?"

"With scripture?" He gave her a dubious look.

"I'm not kidding." She told him what had happened as he drew her into his arms and brushed away her tears.

"Sweet Juli," he said. "Once they think about it and understand, it will work out. If God wants to bless you with a new career, then He knows exactly how to do it."

"Trust in the Lord," she said, realizing how little she trusted even her heavenly Father. "Thanks. It's so easy to try to handle everything myself."

"That's just your way. Our way. I'm guilty, too." He took her hands in his, leaned back, and broke into song to the tune of "Oh, Susanna." "Oh, Juliana, oh, don't you cry for me, 'cause I come from—"

She pulled away and gave him a poke in the side. "Don't make fun."

"But it's so cute." He pulled her into his arms. "So what's happening now?"

"My parents want us to eat with them at the festival. I reminded her you don't eat—"

"Everyone eats garlic at the garlic festival. Anyway, how can we say no? You're already in hot water. Maybe my being around you will keep things calm."

"Would you do that for me?"

"I told you. I'd climb a mountain."

She threw her arms around his neck. "But that's probably lots easier than dealing with my dad."

೭ఎ

Alan had never seen Christmas Hill Park before, but today it appeared to hold the population of Monterey. He'd had a difficult time finding a parking space, and they'd had to walk to the park since many of the roads were barricaded. He slipped his hand into Juli's as they headed inside.

"I can't believe this many people like garlic."

"Everyone likes a party."

He squeezed her hand. "True." He glanced at the throng, wondering if they might have lost her parents. He'd so longed to talk with her today and tell her he was a physician, but adding to her stress now didn't make good sense.

He'd begun to understand why she'd been so hesitant to change her career or even discuss it with her parents. They didn't understand that one person's treasure was someone else's junk. A poor analogy, he knew, but it worked for him.

"I told Mom we'd meet them by the Garlic Garden booth. Dad hangs around there a lot anyway, schmoozing."

He grinned. "Makes sense to meet there," he said, letting her pull him along. "In all the confusion I forgot to ask how things worked out with Megan."

"She's okay. We talked about a lot of things. She's confused, but I hope she's on the right track. I brought up God's expectations and His blessings. She really listened."

"I'm glad." He slipped his arm around her waist and held her close.

"But it gets more interesting. Megan called me this morning."

"What happened?"

"You'll never believe this."

He looked at her dubious expression. "Believe what?"

"Last night Tom sent her a huge bouquet of flowers—roses and orchids. She said she'd never seen such an arrangement, except at a funeral."

Alan chuckled at the description but not at the news. "He told me yesterday he'd made a mistake. I didn't know what to think. I've never heard Tom talk like that."

"Really?" She put on a playful pout. "And you didn't tell me."

He shrugged. "I didn't want to get your hopes up. I never know what to expect from Tom." He patted her hand. "What did Megan say?"

"She had mixed feelings, I think. She was flattered but doubtful it could make a difference. Trust is trust."

"It is," he said, his own messy situation coming to mind. Next week he was on overtime again, and he knew he had to broach the subject of his career. "It's odd how something that seems so unimportant can become so important."

"Trust? You think that's unimportant?"

"No. I didn't mean that. I meant sometimes—"

"I'm teasing." She smiled and pointed ahead. "The vendors are this way."

Alan decided to let the topic drop. This wasn't the time, and it was probably for the best. Maybe today if they found a quiet spot, they could talk. She spoke about trust often, and he had no doubt not telling her would also be a trust issue. He needed time to explain.

As they wended their way through the crowd, Alan spotted five young ladies with tiaras and long gowns—the garlic queen and her court, he assumed. "Look." He pointed through the mob. "That was you a few years ago." He actually felt proud.

"No, that's the real Miss Gilroy Garlic Festival Queen and the runners-up."

He drew back. "That's not the same queen you were back then."

"Right. I was the high school garlic queen. I participated during the crowning of the real Gilroy Garlic Festival Queen. I wasn't eighteen yet, and you have to be for this contest. Anyway, this one is based on an interview, talent, evening gown, and a speech—like a beauty contest. That's not me."

"What do you mean? You have tons of talent. I think you're gorgeous, and I've never seen you in an evening gown, but I'd love to."

"What about the speech?"

He wrapped his arm around her shoulders and drew her to his side. "You make me smile, Juli. I love. . .the way you can do that." He'd swallowed the word that seemed so logical.

As Juli maneuvered her way through the crowd, Alan followed. Stands had been erected displaying everything from wooden and metal crafts to handcrafted jewelry, leatherwork, and dried flowers, and ahead he saw braids of garlic. Finally they entered the food area with ice cream, strawberry desserts, garlic cookbooks, souvenirs, and root beer floats. When he spotted the sign announcing the Garlic Garden, Juli hesitated.

"There they are." She gave him a plaintive look. "I hope my mother didn't say anything about the brochures. I'll be able to tell, and I'll really be irked if she did."

Alan understood but wanted to avoid any confrontation, especially here. "Think positive. Just be yourself."

She gave him a feeble grin then charged off, waving as if nothing were wrong, and her father waved back, a smile lighting his face.

"There's my girl," he said then extended his hand toward Alan. "Good to see you again."

"Thank you, sir. I've looked forward to today." Not to eat garlic, he added to himself, but to see Juli.

"Alan, this is my brother, Jim." Juli motioned to the man standing inside the garlic booth.

"Jim," Alan said, extending his hand. "It's nice to meet you."

"Same here," he said with a crooked smile. "I hear you've been spending time with my little sister."

Juli shook her head. "You sound like Dad, except I'm his little girl."

Alan ignored the banter. "Yes, I've been enjoying your sister's company."

"I heard you met at a soup kitchen in Monterey."

"True. Juli trained me on my first night, and that was the beginning of a great friendship."

Jim chuckled. "Friendship?"

Juli shook her fist. "Stop teasing, Jim. Yes, friendship."

"No fighting, kids," her father said, chuckling. He turned to Alan and made a sweeping gesture toward the surroundings then back to his stand. "What do you think of the place?"

Alan eyed the braids of garlic, bins of garlic buds, and jars of something he assumed contained garlic. "Unbelievable." That was also true. He couldn't believe how many people flocked to the park to celebrate something he'd avoided for so long.

Mr. Maretti patted his belly and eyed his wife. "Ready to eat?"

"We're ready," Juli said, her expression still cautious.

Her father turned to Jim. "You're okay for a while?"

"Fine, Dad. Have fun. And, Alan, I'll set you straight later. You know, give you the lowdown on my sister."

"I can't wait," Alan said, giving him a thumbs-up as they stepped away, pleased to see the brother was a nice guy and Juli held no resentment that he could see.

They walked a short distance until Juli's father stopped and gestured toward the booths. "Who wants to get what?"

Alan noticed Juli studying her mother, who seemed very quiet. He hoped, for Juli's sake, her mom had kept the brochures to herself.

"Can we look around?" Alan whispered to Juli.

She shrugged. "Dad's hungry." She moved closer to her father. "Alan and I'll look around. He's never been here."

"Well, hurry back. The lines are long already."

Alan and Juli dashed through the stands as if they were taking a crash course in home economics while he tried to calculate which food he dared try. When he and Juli returned, each was sent to a different booth to purchase food for the group. Alan stood in the line for barbeque ribs and sandwiches, while Juli headed for the lemonade stand. Her mother had been assigned corn on the cob, and Mr. Maretti had suggested Thai food.

Music spilled from the amphitheater as they made their way to the picnic area, and when they spotted a family leaving a table, Alan rushed ahead to claim it. Their purchases were shifted and moved so everyone could reach them, and finally they bowed their heads as Juli's father asked the blessing.

Alan took a bite of his sandwich, followed by a few fries. Fearing the items were loaded with garlic, he waited a moment to see if he sensed any reaction, but perceiving nothing, he dug in.

Two passersby approached their table, and Mr. Maretti scooted from the bench, his voice booming his greeting. Juli's mother joined him, and grasping the moment alone, Alan slipped his hand in Juli's. "What do you think? It's going okay, don't you think?"

She nodded. "He doesn't know yet."

Alan pressed her hand. "I'm glad. It's hard to believe this caused such excitement."

"Told ya," she said, her voice playful yet disheartened.

Alan nibbled at a pork rib, hoping he and Juli could get away to spend time alone; but in another minute the friends said good-bye, and Juli's parents sat back down on the picnic bench.

Silence filled the air a moment, and Alan sensed tension.

"Do you want to tell your father about the brochures?"

Her mother's voice struck Alan like a dart coming from nowhere.

"What brochures?" Her dad's face filled with question. "A new idea for the store?"

Juli looked as if she wished she could shrink into the picnic bench. Her eyes snapped fire, and she sat with her mouth half open as if she could find no words.

Alan swung his leg over the bench, unwilling to stay and witness the private family discussion.

"Nothing for the business, Dad," Juli said, irritation in her voice. "Just some brochures I was looking at for me."

Her dad did a double take, looking at his wife and then at Juli again. "What kind of brochures?"

"College classes."

A heavy frown settled on his face. "Your brother handles all the business matters, Juli."

"I know, Dad."

"Then you don't really need classes, do you?"

Alan patted Juli's hand. "I'll take a walk."

Juli stiffened. "Mom, why did you do this today?"

"Do what? You said you'd planned to talk to us."

Juli's face sank with discouragement as she looked at Alan. "You don't have to go."

"It's best. I'll be back."

As he stood, he could hear Juli's volume rise. "Mom, Alan's here, and we were having a nice day. I don't understand your reasoning."

"I don't understand yours," was the last thing Alan heard Juli's mother say. He headed toward the music. He didn't want to abandon Juli, but he didn't want her to be mortified by his witnessing a family argument.

twelve

Juli sensed movement behind her and felt Alan's hand touch her shoulder.

"How did it go?"

The confrontation flashed through her mind. "It could have been worse, I guess."

"Really?" He slid onto the bench. "What happened?"

"Daddy was angry at first, but I told him I'd waited to talk to them until I had a clear picture of how I could attend school and still be part of the business."

"For now."

His understanding covered her like a balm. "For now, but I didn't say that. I think it was understood. He appreciates my consideration, but naturally he's dubious about a new career."

"You expected that."

"I did, but I chuckled to myself because afterward he kept telling me how long it would take to get a degree. I think he figures I'll get discouraged and give up so it won't be a problem."

"And will you?"

"I don't think so. I really don't." She wove her fingers through his. "Now that it's in the open, it feels real to me, and I'm excited. I know it'll be difficult and stressful, but anything that's important makes it worthwhile."

He nodded as if he understood. "So where do you go from here?"

"I need to apply and see what happens. I was a good student. I think I'll be admitted with no problem."

"I agree." Alan drew closer, and his gaze searched hers. "Are we alone finally?"

Juli glanced at her watch. "Dad asked me if we were going

to the amphitheater for the next show. It's swing music. He gets a kick out of the dancers. I hated to say no after the fiasco, so I told him we'd find them there. I think we'd better go." She saw disappointment in Alan's eyes.

He rose and offered his hand as she climbed from the picnic bench. He didn't say anything but slipped his arm around her waist. She nestled her head against his shoulder a moment, wanting to kiss him so badly, but the picnic area was filled with people, and she resisted the desire.

They headed toward the music event in silence, Juli thinking about the fracas and Alan apparently thinking about something else. She knew he was disappointed.

"I didn't mean to abandon you earlier," Alan said, his comment unexpected now that the subject had dropped. "I thought you'd be more comfortable, but after I walked away, I hoped you wouldn't think I didn't care or didn't want to support you."

"I understood. I would have been uncomfortable if I'd been in your shoes, too."

"They're too big for you."

She chuckled, remembering her earlier shoe comment. Her spirit lightened, knowing they'd make the best they could of the day. Any time with Alan seemed magical.

When her cell phone sang a tune in her shoulder bag, she stopped. "Who could that be?"

"If you'd answer it, you'd—"

She bumped him with her hip and finished his teasing comment. "I'd know." The phone struck her fingertips as she dug through her purse. She pulled it out and glanced at the caller. "It's Megan. I hope nothing's wrong." She flipped open the phone and answered.

"Tom sent me another huge bouquet of flowers with a note. He wants to see me. What should I do?"

Juli bit her lip then glanced at Alan and mouthed what Megan had said.

He shrugged. "It's up to her."

"Megan, listen to your heart and do what you think is best, but I want you to remember that going slow is better than racing into a problem."

"I know. My heart wants to see him, but I don't know if I can trust him anymore."

"Tell him that. Tell him you'll be on a slow track. If he's willing to wait, and I mean *wait*, then your question has been answered. Jesus told us to forgive if a person repents. Give him a chance to do that."

"Thanks, Juli. You're the best friend anyone could ask for. I should have listened to you weeks ago."

"That's the past. This is the future."

"I love you," Megan said.

"Love you, too." She flipped the phone closed and dropped it into her bag with the words *I love you* ringing in her head. She longed to say those words to Alan, but she wanted to take her own advice. *Take things slowly. Love doesn't run away. It grows and is nourished by patience and thoughtfulness.*

She slipped her arm around Alan's back and smiled at him. When he grinned back, her heart started to swing just like the music that filled the air from the amphitheater.

&

The heat of the kitchen smothered Juli as she walked through the back doorway. Why on such a hot day were they frying meat? She passed the large pots filled with tomato sauce then spotted the fried hamburger. Spaghetti. She managed to smile at the people she passed, knowing her bad mood wasn't anyone's fault. The confrontation with her parents lingered in her mind, and today she knew Alan wouldn't be there either, and that always disappointed her. Next week he'd be back on his regular shift, and that gave her something to look forward to.

Bill strode toward her, and she recognized the need for a favor on his face. She eyed the sauce, and her heart sank. Not today.

"Hi," he said, giving her a bright smile. "Can you handle the sauce? We're shorthanded. You know how it is in the summer. I started browning the meat."

Juli eyed the simmering sauce, its steam misting the air, and nodded. Bill had always been kind, and today she couldn't refuse him the favor, no matter how stressed she felt. She turned down the flame under the burner, slid the huge pan to the back, and emptied a large block of ground beef into the new pot. Someone had diced onions, and as the meat sizzled, she added them to the mix.

Dill slipped behind her and rested his hand on her shoulder. "You got the hot job. Want to trade?"

Though she always suspected Dill had an ulterior motive, his offer seemed genuine. "No, it's okay. Bill asked me, and I can do it."

"I don't mind. Really."

She shook her head and brushed the perspiration from her forehead with her arm. "I love making spaghetti." Her tone had a facetious ring to it.

"I bet." He chuckled. "If Bill asks you to dole it out later, I'll take over then."

She agreed and concentrated on browning the ground beef.

As always, Alan filled her thoughts. She'd recognized his frustration on Saturday when they had no time alone, and between that and the upsetting talk with her parents, she didn't blame him for having a strange look on his face. She'd thought he wanted to tell her something or ask her a question, but he never did, so she'd decided it was her imagination.

Megan had called again on Sunday and said she was having dinner with Tom. Monday when she called, she told Juli he'd apologized and given her a gift, a gold necklace with a heart pendant.

"Will you wear it?" Juli had asked and was happy to hear Megan had thanked him but asked him to keep the gift until she knew what she wanted to do. Juli praised God for Megan's courage. The difference in her actions today compared to a week ago seemed a 180-degree turn. The most surprising news was that Tom accepted her offer and promised he would prove himself worthy.

The meat's sizzle drew Juli back to her work, and she lifted the heavy skillet, poured some of the grease off then spooned the meat into the sauce. Her hand trembled from its weight, and she hurried to empty the pot before she dropped it. With a relieved sigh, she set it down.

She turned off the burner on the second pot and lifted it; but this time her arm couldn't keep the weight steady, and grease splashed from the pan to the floor. She looked around for help then spotted Dill and called to him. As he bounded toward her, she nodded toward the floor. "I spilled grease. Be careful!" she yelled so everyone could heed her warning.

"You want me to wipe it up?"

"First could you hold the pan while I empty the meat into the sauce? I did the first pot, but this one is too heavy."

He lifted the kettle, and she used the large spoon to scoop the meat into the other pot of sauce and give it a stir. "Thanks."

He lowered the pot to the counter. "Anything else?" He gave her a wink.

"No, I'm fine. Thanks." When he stepped away, she rolled her eyes, recognizing one of Dill's toying come-ons. As she moved to stir the meat into the sauce, Juli felt her foot slip on the greasy floor. She tried to catch herself, but the hot burner seemed her only choice. Instead she reached for the center island without success. She lost her balance, her ankle twisted, and she tumbled to the floor. Pain shot up her leg, and a groan escaped her. She heard a gasp from others. Before she could move, Bill reached her side.

Gritting her teeth, she pressed her hands against the floor to rise, but he knelt beside her, holding her in place.

"Don't get up," he said with such authority he sounded like her father.

"Why?" Although she kept her voice steady, her hand trembled as panic gripped her.

"I want to check your ankle. You might have broken it."

"I'm fine." She waved him away.

"Let me decide that."

"Should I call you Dr. Bill?" She tried to grin, but she knew her expression looked more like a grimace.

Bill didn't smile back. "Someone put ice in a plastic bag."

"I'm okay. Really." While she said the words, a sharp pain charged up her leg, and she couldn't hold back the moan that followed.

Bill rose, his hand spread over her as if holding back a lion. "I'm not sure if it's sprained or broken, but we're not taking any chances. I'll call 911."

"911? Please—that's ridiculous. I can walk, and I'm not going to the hospital in an ambulance."

Dill stepped forward. "Would you go to the hospital if we can get you into a car?"

Juli stopped fighting. Her ankle throbbed, and she felt miserable. She'd bumped her shoulder when she fell, and she was sure she would have a horrible bruise. "Okay. I give up."

Bill thought a moment and dug in his pockets for the keys. "Put her in my car right outside the door, and I'll be there in a minute. I'll get Randy to take over." He tossed Dill the keys and hurried away.

Dill helped her get up while another young man moved in, and together they made a seat with their arms and lifted Juli off the ground. She felt like a child on a swing, except for pain rolling from her foot up her leg.

Juli clung to their shoulders. Once she was settled in Bill's car with the ice bag tied around her ankle, she leaned against the headrest and tried to control the pain pulsing along her limb. *So dumb,* she thought as she recalled how she'd warned everyone else of the grease.

Bill slipped into the car and started the engine while Juli

closed her eyes. "Would you mind taking me to Community Hospital in Monterey? Alan's working tonight, and—"

"It'll take a few minutes longer, but I can manage that."

She felt ridiculous asking, but she wanted to be with Alan, and she hoped she would see him there.

Bill pulled out of the parking lot and switched on the radio to a blues station. The music lilted her into a calm as she sent up a prayer that the Lord would bless her injury with an uncomplicated diagnosis like a simple sprain. Anything but a break.

Bill hummed along to an old tune, and she let her mind wander, thinking of the past couple of weeks and all that had happened. Tonight Megan and Tom hadn't been at the soup kitchen, and now they would be very shorthanded with her mess-up.

When Bill's voice jolted her, she wondered if she'd fallen asleep. He'd turned into the emergency entrance of the hospital and slowed to a stop near the door. In moments she was helped into a wheelchair and taken through the wide double doors, where she presented her insurance information and was wheeled to the side to wait.

As she felt her chair move and saw an aide behind her, Bill came through the door and signaled he'd wait in the lounge. Poor Bill, getting waylaid by her carelessness. She nodded to him, wishing she had someone else and thinking of Megan, who lived close by. If she could come and give her a ride back to her car, then Bill could return to the soup kitchen.

"Could I make one call?" she asked over her shoulder.

The aide shrugged, so she took that as a yes and opened her bag to find her cell phone. Megan answered. "Don't panic. I'm in emergency at Community Hospital right here in Monterey."

"Emergency?"

Before Megan lost it, Juli told her what had happened. "I'd like to send Bill back to the kitchen. They're really shorthanded, and I thought maybe you could drive me back to my car unless you're not feeling well."

"I'm fine. Just tired, but I'm not too tired to come. I'll hurry over."

Confident Megan would be there, Juli asked the aide to send someone to the waiting room and tell Bill she had a friend on the way so he could leave. She looked at the clock, longing to get into a room and learn what was wrong. Sitting there wasn't accomplishing anything but making her more nervous.

The aide returned and in a moment whisked her through the doors and settled her inside a curtained cubicle. He walked away without a word. She sat, waiting and glancing at her watch until finally a nurse entered with a million questions and took her vital signs. A male nurse joined her and helped Juli onto the table. They left and slid the curtain closed.

Juli wished she'd thought to ask for Alan or at least asked one of them to let him know she was there. Time dragged, and she wondered if Megan had arrived yet. Finally she heard sounds outside the curtain, the fabric slipped back, and Alan stepped inside. Juli watched his face shift from one expression to another until he seemed to accept that she was sitting there on the examination table.

"What happened to you?" His gaze shifted over her frame like a searchlight, apparently noticing the slight redness on her arm but ending up on her swollen ankle.

Seeing him in a lab coat sent her pulse on a jog. He looked so handsome and professional. "I slipped on grease. Really stupid. I'm sure it's nothing, but Bill insisted on bringing me here."

"Why here?" He frowned. "You'd have been closer if—"

The look wasn't what she'd expected. "I knew you were working. I asked him to come here."

"Let me take a look."

His concern was riddled with another expression she couldn't understand. "Maybe I made a mistake. I wanted to see you."

He pulled gloves from a box on the wall and tugged them on as he moved to her ankle.

When he touched it, she tried to control a moan but without success.

"Can you point your toe upward?"

She forced it up, trying to cover the stabbing ache. He had her move it right and left. The movement sent pulses throbbing through her foot.

"It hurts here?" he asked, probing the area.

She tried not to groan. "Maybe it's just a little sprain."

He raised his head. "It's not a little anything until we get some X-rays. It's probably a second-degree sprain, but you could have a fracture."

Even with the throbbing, she couldn't avoid being amused. "Who do you think you are? A doctor?"

When he lifted his head, he didn't smile, and her gaze moved to the ID tag on his lab coat. *Alan Louden, MD, Community Hospital of the Monterey Peninsula.* She felt as if she'd been punched in the stomach and then dropped three floors in an elevator. MD? But she thought he was a nurse. A multitude of emotions washed over her. Confusion. Disappointment. Pride. Her focus adhered to the ID tag. "You're a doctor? You told me you were a nurse."

His face tensed as he gave her a brief nod without looking at her. "I didn't, Juli. I told you I nursed patients, and I do."

She searched his eyes, wanting more answers. "How many times have I asked you about your day? You just told me you were busy with a motorcycle accident or a child's broken arm or someone with a dog bite or someone with an allergic reaction. When I asked you where you went to school, you told me University of California at San Francisco. They have a huge nursing program there."

His head lowered. "They have a medical program, too, Juli. I'm sorry."

"Is Tom a doctor, too?"

His eyes shifted from her ankle to her face. "No, he's a nurse." He shook his head. "It's a long story, Juli, and I tried to tell you a few times, but something always got in the way."

"Got in the way? Of something this significant?" The word *trust* knifed through her. Why would he hide part of his life from her? How could she trust him now? What other secrets did he have?

"I'm sorry, Juli." He leaned over her. "Could we talk about this later? I want to arrange for X-rays, and we're really busy tonight."

Before she could respond, he slipped through the curtain and vanished.

Physician? Medical doctor? She had pictured him as a nurse but never a doctor. She shook her head, trying to imagine his reasons for not telling her. Had he felt sorry for her never going to college? Had their relationship been that shallow? She couldn't believe it.

She closed her eyes, willing herself not to make a rash decision. She needed to hear his explanation.

While her mind raced, the curtain parted again, and another aide arrived to take her for X-rays. Alan hadn't returned, and she felt confused beyond words. She'd gotten involved too fast. She'd given Megan advice about the same thing, but she hadn't heeded her own warning. As the aide wheeled her down the corridor, she had to fight back her tears.

Juli was shifted and jiggled while the technician took the X-rays, and then a different aide arrived to take her back. When she returned to emergency, he set her beside the wall in the corridor. She heard Alan's voice float from a cubicle, but Juli couldn't see him. Did she want to? Her heart told her yes, but her confusion told her no. When Alan found her in the hall, a nurse joined them, leaving Juli no time to ask questions other than inquiries about her ankle.

"The X-rays show no fracture, Juli, but sometimes it can take up to fourteen days to show a hairline fracture. We won't hold you here, but you need to stay off that foot and keep it elevated to help prevent any more swelling. Compression is important, so I'll have someone wrap it before you leave, and you'll need to use crutches. You can get instructions on using them at a medical supply store. Understand?"

He sounded so formal and professional that Juli felt as if she couldn't relate to him. Where was the Alan she'd come here to see, the one who would empathize with her pain and kiss it away? She wanted a signal to show he cared.

"Juli? Do you understand?"

She fought the tears welling in her eyes. "Yes, I understand."

"I want you to ice the area with a cold pack at least twice a day for about fifteen minutes, and I'll give you a prescription for pain medication. If it hasn't improved in two or three days, then we'll need to check for a hairline fracture." He pulled out a prescription pad, and as he jotted on it, another nurse appeared.

"Someone is here to pick you up," she said.

Alan glanced at her with curiosity.

"It's Megan." Juli turned to the nurse. "Thanks."

Alan tore off two sheets, and as he handed them to her, the two nurses walked away.

Juli glanced at the prescription sheets, unable to make sense out of the squiggle. Had she seen his penmanship before, she might have realized he was a physician from the illegible scrawl. "What are these for?"

"Pain medication, and the other is for the medical supply store for the crutches and some compression wraps."

Her gaze locked with his, and for one moment she saw a flicker of the Alan she'd grown to love.

"I'm sorry about this, Juli."

"It wasn't your fault. I slipped on the grease."

He touched her arm. "No, I mean about your learning I'm a doctor this way."

Her throat constricted, and her response tangled in a knot. She shook her head.

Behind Alan she saw an aide arriving with a wheelchair. Alan and the young man helped her into it and adjusted her feet on the footrest.

Alan's gaze probed hers. "I'll call you later."

Anger loosened her voice. "I thought it was 'Take an aspirin and call me in the morning.'"

His expression looked as if she'd slapped him.

Silence fell between them, and the aide unlocked the brake and pushed her down the corridor toward the emergency room exit. She prayed Megan was waiting for her alone. With her heart in her throat, she needed a friend who'd understand how much it hurt to lose trust in someone.

thirteen

Alan looked at the food choices in the cafeteria and walked past. Instead he grabbed a soda from the cooler, paid the cashier, and found a table in the back corner where he hoped he could be alone. He'd tried Juli's cell twice and her home phone once. She didn't answer, and he'd left messages in both places. Was she ignoring him or staying with her parents? Even if she was there, she had her cell phone. She never went anywhere without that.

He popped open the tab on the soda and took a long drink, then put his elbows on the table and lowered his face in his hands. The long shifts had worn him thin and thrown his system out of whack. Now to have this situation with Juli was almost more than he could handle.

Deciding to give her another try, Alan flipped open the cell and pressed the button with her number coded in. "Please answer," he said aloud as he slipped it to his ear and listened. Nothing but the telephone voice telling him to leave a message. He'd done that. He slapped the phone closed and slid it into his pocket.

Alan knew he'd made a mistake not telling Juli, but when he'd tried to rectify it before the last unbelievable situation, he'd failed. Something always happened. Interruptions. Bad timing. Lack of good sense. That was his problem from the beginning. He closed his eyes and talked to the Lord, asking Him how to solve the situation. *Trust in God.* The words rang clear in his head, and a verse he'd learned so long ago entered his thoughts. He suspected he didn't have the words exact, but it was close enough to remind him of God's promises. *"Trust in God all the time and open your hearts to Him, because God is our refuge.*" Alan trusted God, and he trusted Juli. Now if only he could convince her to have confidence in him.

He opened his eyes and pulled the phone from his pocket. One more try couldn't hurt. He pushed the button. The computerized message sounded in his ears. "Your call has been forwarded to an automatic voice answering system." He closed the cell phone.

Giving up wasn't in Alan's vocabulary. Tomorrow he'd call, and the next day, and the next. Flowers worked for Tom. He'd buy Juli so many flowers she wouldn't know where to put them. He shook his head. Juli cared about him, he was certain, and if God had a part in their meeting and their lives, He would bless their relationship. Juli had to listen to his reasoning.

৯

Juli waved good-bye to Megan from the top of her apartment staircase, leaning on crutches, while her mother hovered behind her.

"You need to get that leg up, Juli," her mother said, holding open the door. "I can't believe you did this. You knew the grease was there."

"I wasn't thinking, Mom." She hobbled into her apartment with more on her mind than her sprained ankle.

Her mother stood beside the recliner. "At least you called me last night. I would have been worried to death."

"It seemed wiser to stay with Megan than to call you and Daddy to drive down and pick me up. I couldn't ask Megan to drive me home and drive back so late at night. And I would have had these stairs to deal with in the dark."

Juli crumpled into the chair, dropped her crutches by her side, and leaned back. "It was a horrible night."

"I'm sure it was." Her mother pivoted then looked back at Juli. "You said you had a prescription."

"It's in my purse."

Without asking, her mother dug into her shoulder bag and

pulled out the prescription bottle and eyed the label. "You're supposed to take one of these every four to six hours for pain."

"I know. I'll need one soon. My ankle's really bothering me."

Her mother set the shoulder bag on the arm of Juli's chair, and Juli moved it to the lamp table. When she looked up, her mother was staring at the bottle. "What's wrong?"

She held the bottle out to Juli and pointed at the label. "This is a coincidence."

"What?"

"A physician named Alan Louden was your ER doctor? Did you realize that?" She lowered the bottle, her eyes widening. "Alan works at Community Hospital of the Monterey Peninsula, doesn't he?"

Juli knew what was coming. She nodded.

"Do you mean to tell me Alan is a physician and you never told me?"

Juli faced her options—tell her mother she didn't know Alan was a doctor either or just agree she'd never told her mother. *Lord, what do I do now?* If her parents knew the truth, they would distrust Alan, and Juli needed time to understand.

"Are you okay?" Her mother stepped closer. "I asked you a question."

Her mind ached nearly as much as her ankle. "Mom, I really need that medicine now."

"I'm sorry," she said, looking confused for a moment. She set the container beside Juli and headed into the kitchen.

Tension knotted Juli's stomach. She didn't want to lie to her mother, but she didn't know how to get out of answering her question. She'd planned to tell her parents, but once again she hadn't had time to decide how. Before her mother returned, Juli's cell phone rang, and she dug into her bag, located it, and flipped it open. Alan's voice floated through the line.

"I'm home from work, Juli. I'm tired, but we need to talk. Can I come over?"

"I'm feeling rotten. I really need to get some rest, Alan. This whole thing has put me in a bad situation with my—"

Her mother strode into the room with the glass of water.

Juli stared at the phone. "My mom's giving me a pain pill."

"I'll hang on, and I understand. I'm sure they're wondering why I didn't say anything either, but I can explain."

"Just a minute." She placed the phone in her lap and opened her hand for the pill then grasped the glass. The pill slid down, and she finished the water before handing her mother the glass and picking up the phone. "Okay, I'm back."

"Can I come?"

Juli eyed her mother, not wanting to call Alan by name because it would remind her of her earlier question. "I need to take a nap. I'll talk with you later." She closed her phone and set it beside her on the lamp table. "Mom, I really need to sleep."

"Let me get you a pillow to put under your leg. Are you hungry?"

"No, Megan made breakfast. I'll eat later."

Her mother scurried from the room and returned with the pillow. She lifted Juli's leg and slid the pillow beneath her calf. "Are you comfortable?"

"It's fine. Thanks." She closed her eyes, hoping her mother would leave.

"I hate leaving you alone. What if you need something?"

"Mom, I have the crutches. I can get up if I must. Leave the door unlocked, and you can get in later, or call me in a couple of hours. I'll be fine."

Her mother leaned over and kissed her cheek as her palm rested on Juli's forehead.

"I don't have a fever."

Her mom pulled her hand away. "I was just checking." She paused then kissed Juli's cheek. "I love you."

"Love you, too, Mom."

Juli opened her eyes a crack and saw her mother creep across the room and exit. Juli's head dropped against the recliner, and she drew in a breath. Tiredness swept over her, but her mind didn't want to rest. Last night she'd talked to Megan until late, thinking about so many things. All Alan's wonderful qualities had filled her mind, but something else had struck her.

She recalled Alan's complimenting her on her bedside manner, as he sometimes called it. She thought he was joking with the terminology because he worked at the hospital. Now it angered her. He was a doctor. He had her teaching him how to talk with people when that was part of his job. Why had he played games with her like that? He'd kept his career a secret and then made her look foolish with his "teach me to be like you" talk. And she'd fallen for it.

No matter where her mind went, it always came back to one truth. She'd fallen in love with Alan, and she didn't want to let him go. Megan shared her experience with Tom. Although Megan and Tom had been separated only a few days, the absence had definitely made a difference in their relationship because they'd found the time to think about what was important. Should she tell Alan not to come when he called again?

❧

Alan stood outside Juli's apartment, holding a bouquet of summer flowers. He'd thought through the reason he hadn't told her, and now his concern seemed as purposeless as a broom on a beach. His chest felt tight as he struggled to draw in air. After willing his hand to move, he pressed the doorbell and waited.

He pictured Juli trying to rise from her seat and maneuver across the room with her crutches. He should have called to tell her he was on his way. When he heard nothing, he faltered outside the door. Was she below with her parents or perhaps asleep? He tried the doorknob and opened it an inch. "Juli?"

Finally he heard her voice. "It's open."

He pushed the door wider and stepped inside. Juli sat in the recliner, her foot propped on a pillow and her eyes heavy with sleep. "I thought maybe you were with your parents."

She shook her head then opened her eyes. They shifted to the flowers. "I didn't know you were coming."

"You said we'd talk later. I realized you couldn't say much because your mother was here."

"I meant I'd talk with you on the phone."

Her comment punctured his balloon of hope. He felt the flowers droop in his arm. "I'm sorry. I misunderstood."

"You're here now." She straightened her back and let the recliner seat lower while keeping her foot elevated.

"These are for you," he said, holding the flowers toward her, feeling as if they were a pitiful token of his apology.

"They're beautiful. Could you find a vase and fill it with water?" She motioned toward the kitchen. "I think I have a couple in a lower cabinet next to the sink."

Alan carried the bouquet into the kitchen, uneasy that he'd showed up unwanted. His mind reeled with her attitude and his bungle. Two bungles, he admitted—not telling her he was a physician and showing up without calling. He crouched beside the cabinet and located a large vase in the back. He rose and filled it with water then pulled off the floral wrapping and dropped the flowers into the vase. He knew there was some kind of art to arranging flowers, but he'd never had to do it before. He drew back then stepped closer and moved a few blossoms from one side to the other, trying to balance height and color.

As he lifted the vase, he noticed the packet of plant food inside the wrapping. He read on the label that it was meant to help the flowers last and sprinkled the food into the water. He wished he had something to sprinkle on his relationship with Juli—if it were only that simple.

He stood in the doorway with the arrangement, feeling as if he should set them on a table and leave, but that would be unproductive. He'd come for a purpose, and he hoped the

Lord would open the door to heal the hurt he'd caused. Juli held her purse in her lap, and he noticed she'd combed her hair and put on lipstick while he was in the kitchen. Her action gave him hope.

"You can set the vase right there," Juli said, pointing to a table beside the doorway.

Alan noticed they looked nice there when he walked away. "I guess I should have called, but when you said we'd talk—"

"It's okay." She motioned to the sofa. "Have a seat."

He wanted to put his arm around her and kiss her, but he saw she wanted distance between them. Still, his doctor persona caused him to move toward her. "Do you mind if I look at your ankle first?"

She looked down then lifted her head. "You're the doctor."

Her barb dug deep, but he went to her anyway, unwrapped her foot, and studied her ankle. "Have you been putting cold compresses on it?"

"Not this morning yet. I was tired when I got home. I stayed with Megan last night, and she brought me home this morning. We stopped on the way for the prescription and to get the crutches. They were out of cold packs."

"Do you mind if I make a compress for you?"

She gestured toward the kitchen without answering.

With her direction he located plastic bags, doubled them, then filled them with ice and carried them back. "How about a hand towel or something to put around it?"

"You'll find them in the bathroom."

He located a towel, came back, and applied the cold pack before he sat on the sofa. "How are you doing with the crutches?"

"It's not easy. Did you count the stairs to get up here?"

"I thought about that." He had so much to talk about, but she seemed too far away, as if a wall had dropped between them. "I know you don't want me here, Juli, but I want to tell you I'm more sorry than you can ever imagine. I know the

Lord forgives, and I hope you can, too. . .in time."

She closed her eyes a moment without saying a word.

"I could give you a million reasons why I wasn't open about what I do at the hospital, but it boils down to my past. I was at the soup kitchen because I felt drawn to help others who are in the same situation my family was in a few years ago. I didn't want to be there as a physician or spend my time diagnosing everyone's illnesses rather than what I went there to do. I wanted to serve people in a different way—as a plain guy who volunteered."

"But you could have told me."

"When we first met, I didn't know how I would come to feel about you, so I was evasive. I never lied. When Tom came to the soup kitchen, I feared he'd say something, so I pledged him to secrecy. That's how important it was to me. I didn't want to be the kindly physician. I wanted to do this as me, the little boy who stood in a soup kitchen line one time when a person gave me a double portion in the same way I asked you to give that child an extra portion one day. Remember?"

Remembrance filled her face.

"After a while I realized I'd messed up. You began talking about trust, especially with Megan and Tom's situation, and I knew you would consider this a trust issue, and I suppose it was. It's not that I don't trust you implicitly, but the more people who know I'm a physician, the easier it is to slip."

"I should have known. You used your doctoring skills when you talked with the people. You saw them always with their health in mind."

"While you looked at them with their souls in mind."

Her forehead wrinkled as she weighed what he'd said. "I suppose that's right, but I'm so hurt that you spent so much time complimenting me on my 'bedside' manner. Bedside manner? That's what doctors have. Why didn't I realize you were patronizing me?"

Alan couldn't remain seated. He stood then knelt beside

her chair. "I wasn't patronizing you. I found your ability for compassion and concern amazing. I'm a good doctor, Juli, but what I lack are bedside manners. I don't look at the person's fears and needs beyond their health. You do. I wanted to learn from you."

She studied his face for a long time, recalling how cold he'd seemed at the hospital. Could this be what he meant? "I need to think about this, Alan."

His fingers itched to weave with hers, to touch her in a loving way, but he held back to respect her wishes. "So where do we go from here?"

"I need to think. I'll have to explain this to my parents. My mother saw your name on the pill container. She won't let her curiosity die until she knows why I never told her you were a doctor."

"And that'll put me on the wrong list." He looked at her face. "If I'm not there already."

She drew in a ragged breath. "Maybe you had a reason you thought was a good one, but it's upset me. I really need time to work this through, and yes, it has to do with trust. I'm not feeling well, and I'm out of patience. . .spelled with a *ce*. Give me some time. Okay?"

Patience spelled with a ce. He wanted to hug her for her lighthearted comment, so much like the good times.

"I'll respect your wishes because I respect you." He rose and pulled his car keys from his pocket. "How long?"

For a moment she looked as if she didn't understand. "Give me a couple of weeks."

A couple of weeks. Impaled to the spot, he let his gaze wash over her a moment. "I not only respect you, Juli. I love you." He turned away, fearing he'd lost the love of his life. He headed to his car filled with regret and emptiness.

fourteen

"I not only respect you. I love you." The words had echoed in Juli's thoughts every day since Alan had walked out the door. She missed him with all her heart.

When she'd finally checked her cell phone, she'd noticed how many times Alan had called the night she'd stayed with Megan. He'd left a message on her home telephone, as well. She'd tossed his reasoning around in her mind, looking at it one way and then another, often accepting what he said then negating it. The issue had grown from the proverbial molehill to a mountain.

Alan had sent her another bouquet, and she wondered if he'd learned that from Tom. Again her trust wavered while she made two steps forward and one back. She'd been more depressed than she could have imagined. She'd talked often with Megan, who had told her Alan was a mess at work.

Yet Alan had kept his promise. He hadn't called in twelve days, but she wished he would. Until the day he walked out, he'd never said he loved her, although her senses told her he did. One thing she knew for sure—she loved him with all her heart. So why had she let this drag on so long?

Because, to Juli, a relationship that seemed to be leading to marriage was to be taken seriously and with thought. She sensed God had led her to Alan, but she wanted to know it was true and not just her own desire. Megan and Tom's relationship had progressed, and it gave her hope. Tom had begun attending church, Megan told her, and they had agreed to go slowly. From what she could tell, they were following the agreement no matter how much human nature tried to take control. Juli guessed they would be engaged before the end of the year.

While recuperating, she'd filled out her application for the university. Her father admitted the store had been surviving well without her being in it every day. She could still do inventory, ordering, scheduling, and overseeing. Computers were amazing.

Juli eased herself from the recliner, but overcome for a moment with dizziness, she grabbed a crutch and steadied herself then made her way into the kitchen. She had graduated from having her mother bring up food to preparing some things on her own. Doing things for herself felt good. When she opened the refrigerator, she felt the room rock. The refrigerator door swung back then slammed shut, hitting her and throwing her off balance. She toppled to the floor. They were having an earthquake, she realized as she struggled to right herself.

Before she'd pulled herself up, her mother's voice sailed from the living room. "Are you okay, Juli?"

"I'm fine, Mom."

Her mother appeared in the kitchen doorway. "It's an aftershock."

"I know. Can you help me up? The refrigerator door whacked me."

On her feet again, Juli made her way back to the living room, where her mother turned on the TV. "How close is it?"

"An earthquake hit Morgan Hill."

"That's only ten miles from Gilroy."

"Hush," her mother said, waving at her.

Juli balanced on her crutch, feeling a rumble that knocked a picture cockeyed on the wall. She made her way to the chair, sat down, and listened to the newscaster.

"The last earthquake measured 4.5 on the Richter scale," he said.

"Let's watch the program downstairs, Mom."

Her mother rose and clicked off the TV. "I want to call

your dad and see if he's okay." She crossed the room to Juli's side. "Let me help you."

As Juli stood, another aftershock rattled through the building and sent the vase of flowers Alan had given her tumbling to the floor.

ঽ

Alan had been counting the days. Only two days to go and he could call Juli, and by then, he prayed, she would forgive him for his error and, most of all, trust him. On working days the time didn't drag as much as it did on his days off. He'd cleaned his apartment twice in the past days, trying to find things to do that would take his time.

How had he spent his time before Juli? He couldn't remember, but he knew his life had revolved around his work with an occasional date that always left him wishing he hadn't gone. Dates seemed to set up expectations, but that had never happened with Juli. They met and fell into step like two old friends who'd been apart but had come together again. They shared so many things. Even their opposites seemed compatible.

Alan sank into his favorite easy chair, stacked the morning paper in a jumble at his feet, and reached for the TV remote. He never watched TV during the day, but he couldn't stand the quiet any longer. He pushed the power button, and as the picture and voice came in, he stared at the screen. A 4.5 earthquake in Morgan Hill. He raised the volume.

"Aftershocks are being felt as far away as Gilroy with some damage being reported in some areas. Let's go live to Ron Brice in Watsonville."

Alan lowered the volume and grabbed his cell phone. He punched in Juli's apartment and heard the answering machine kick in. He hung up and tried her cell phone. The phone rang three times followed by the voice-mail message. "Where are you?" he yelled into the air. He waited a moment, knowing it still took Juli awhile to get to the phone, and tried the numbers again. Nothing. She didn't answer.

He snapped off the TV. He didn't care how many days he was supposed to wait. If she didn't answer, then he was going to her. He wouldn't take a chance. Alan dashed from his apartment, jumped into his car, and headed up Highway 1 through Castorville then took Highway 101 toward Gilroy. He switched on the radio and listened to the news accounts— one bridge was down and a few buildings damaged. He pushed the button for another station.

Traffic slowed going into Gilroy, and he took a cutoff to Juli's house, hoping he'd made the right decision. When he arrived, everything looked normal, but as he stepped from the car, he felt the rumble from an aftershock and waited for it to pass. He darted toward the staircase and rang Juli's bell. He tried the door and opened it, calling as he did. No sound.

He ran down the steps and headed for her parents' front door. Before he rang the bell, Mrs. Maretti pulled it open. "She's in the family room, Alan."

"I'm sorry, but I heard about the earthquake, and I—"

Her mother nodded silently and gestured down the hall.

"Thank you." He hurried past the open staircase and stepped through the family room archway.

Juli was seated in an easy chair, her leg propped on an ottoman, but her back was straining forward. He guessed she'd heard his voice. Now that he was here, he felt foolish. "I was worried," he said, his voice sounding hollow in his ears. "Are you okay?"

She shook her head no, and he faltered. "What is it?" He shifted to her side.

"I miss you," she said, tears brimming in her eyes.

He knelt beside her. "And I've missed you so much."

She opened her arms, and he fell into her embrace. Her tears dampened his cheek as he drew her as close as he could, whispering all the things he'd held in his heart for so long. Finally he pulled back and looked into her shining eyes.

"Do you forgive me?"

"Do you forgive me?"

They needed no answer. He clasped her hands in his then wove his fingers through hers, something he'd longed to do since the day he'd walked away from her door feeling empty.

"I understand," she said, running her finger from his jaw to his lips.

He kissed her finger and held it there so he could kiss it once more. "Let's never let this happen again." He lowered his hand and brushed her cheek.

"Never," she agreed. "My devotional today really spoke to me."

"What did it say?"

" 'Let the morning bring me word of Your unfailing love, for I have put my trust in You.' I realized by trusting God I can also trust you with my whole heart, because He gave you to me in an amazing way. There we were at a soup kitchen, a place for giving to others, and that day the Lord gave me you."

"And today I promise you my unfailing love."

His lips met hers in the sweetest kiss she could ever remember, and when he drew back, she kissed him again. Kisses were meant for love, and so were they.

epilogue

The following June

As Megan adjusted Juli's wedding veil, Juli stood in the bride's room and watched the beads wink in the sunlight streaming through the window. She loved the fitted bodice with more beadwork and the flow of the white dress around her feet. As a little girl, she'd longed to be a bride, and today her dream was coming true.

She turned toward the door, expecting her mother to appear any minute with their wedding bouquets and last-minute instructions. She knew it would be another time for tears, but now she wept tears of joy. She couldn't believe how amazingly her life had evolved; even her sprained ankle last July had given her dad proof the Garlic Garden could get along without her. She'd begun her classes in late August the previous year, and on her birthday she and Alan had become engaged. He'd given her a beautiful wristwatch as a birthday gift, and beneath the box's velvet lining he'd hidden the marquis diamond engagement ring that had now been mounted into a gold filigree ring jacket to form her wedding band.

Everything had flown by before her eyes, meeting Alan's wonderful mother then later his brother, who was to be their best man, and his sister. Juli couldn't wait to meet his other sisters when she and Alan honeymooned on the East Coast.

"You're absorbed in something."

Megan's voice jolted her back to the present, and she turned from the door to face her longtime friend. "I'm thinking how fast the time has flown since my engagement." She gazed at Megan's floor-length gown in summer green with a cummerbund waist of embroidered pastel flowers. The gown looked perfect with her blond hair and slender frame. "You look lovely, and it won't be long before your wedding."

"Soon, but today it's yours."

Her sweet smile touched Juli. "I'm happy for you and Tom. See what God can do when you give Him a chance."

Megan nodded. "And when you do it His way. Look what the Lord has done with Tom. He's become a Christian man with a new heart, Christian morals, and new goals."

They embraced, and as they parted, Juli recognized her mother's quiet rap on the door. She came into the room, her eyes moist with happiness. "Everything's so beautiful, and the church is packed."

Concern skittered up Juli's arms. "Didn't the flowers come yet?"

Her mother smiled. "Your dad is bringing them to you. He wants to be here."

Tear's blurred Juli's eyes as another soft tap on the door answered her question. When her mother opened it, her father walked in with Megan's bouquet resting on top of a floral box. Juli grasped the maid of honor's flowers and handed them to her.

Megan gazed at the blossoms then at the similar smaller design adorning her waist. "Perfect. This is beautiful."

Her father held the floral box and looked at Juli. "This isn't exactly what you ordered."

Her father had been trying to hide his grin, but his comment concerned her. "What do you mean?"

"Alan bought these flowers especially for you."

"Alan?" Juli lifted the box lid and let out a little cry. On top of the tissue she found a card written in Alan's peculiar scrawl. *"Special flowers for a special lady. When all else fails we can laugh our cares away."* They had certainly done that, but the cryptic message added to her curiosity. She pushed back the tissue, and inside lay an arrangement of white roses with sprigs of long-stemmed scarpes, delicate white flowers on curling stems, and small lavender allium, both grown from garlic bulbs. Tears blurred her eyes. "He's amazing."

As she pulled the bouquet from the box, her father's chuckle greeted her. "It's a rose and garlic bouquet."

She held the arrangement against her beaded dress. "But this one I love."

"I thought you would." He stepped to her side and kissed her cheek. "We'd better get out there, little girl."

He grasped her arm, and today she loved hearing him call her his little girl. Sometimes she was. "Let's go, Daddy."

Her mother and Megan left first, and Juli held back as the others went down the aisle. When the "Trumpet Voluntary" began, she knew it was her cue, and she and her father moved into the archway and began the long walk down the aisle. Ahead of her she could see Alan, looking so handsome she could hardly contain herself. His blond hair appeared even blonder against his black tuxedo, and those dusky periwinkle eyes she loved followed her as she walked toward him.

At the front her father released her to Alan's care and settled beside her mother, and the pastor began, his words wrapping around her heart.

Alan squeezed her hand, and she heard him murmur, "You're too beautiful for words." Today she felt that way. As they spoke their vows, she saw the sun stream through the magnificent stained-glass windows and tint her dress with its hues. To her it was the Lord's way of sending His blessing as she stood beside the man God had given her to respect, love, honor, and trust always.

A Letter To Our Readers

Dear Reader:

In order that we might better contribute to your reading enjoyment, we would appreciate your taking a few minutes to respond to the following questions. We welcome your comments and read each form and letter we receive. When completed, please return to the following:

Fiction Editor
Heartsong Presents
PO Box 719
Uhrichsville, Ohio 44683

1. Did you enjoy reading *Garlic and Roses* by Gail G. Martin?
   ☐ Very much! I would like to see more books by this author!
   ☐ Moderately. I would have enjoyed it more if

   _____

   _____

   _____

2. Are you a member of **Heartsong Presents**? ☐ Yes ☐ No
   If no, where did you purchase this book? _____

   _____

3. How would you rate, on a scale from 1 (poor) to 5 (superior), the cover design? _____

4. On a scale from 1 (poor) to 10 (superior), please rate the following elements.

   ____ Heroine   ____ Plot
   ____ Hero   ____ Inspirational theme
   ____ Setting   ____ Secondary characters

5. These characters were special because? _____
_____
_____

6. How has this book inspired your life? _____
_____
_____

7. What settings would you like to see covered in future
   Heartsong Presents books? _____
_____
_____

8. What are some inspirational themes you would like to see
   treated in future books? _____
_____
_____

9. Would you be interested in reading other **Heartsong
   Presents** titles? ❏ Yes ❏ No

10. Please check your age range:
   ❏ Under 18   ❏ 18-24
   ❏ 25-34   ❏ 35-45
   ❏ 46-55   ❏ Over 55

Name_____
Occupation_____
Address_____
City, State, Zip_____

Presents

__HP673	*Flash Flood*, D. Mills
__HP677	*Banking on Love*, J. Thompson
__HP678	*Lambert's Peace*, R. Hauck
__HP681	*The Wish*, L. Bliss
__HP682	*The Grand Hotel*, M. Davis
__HP685	*Thunder Bay*, B. Loughner
__HP686	*Always a Bridesmaid*, A. Boeshaar
__HP689	*Unforgettable*, J. L. Barton
__HP690	*Heritage*, M. Davis
__HP693	*Dear John*, K. V. Sawyer
__HP694	*Riches of the Heart*, T. Davis
__HP697	*Dear Granny*, P. Griffin
__HP698	*With a Mother's Heart*, J. Livingston
__HP701	*Cry of My Heart*, L. Ford
__HP702	*Never Say Never*, L. N. Dooley
__HP705	*Listening to Her Heart*, J. Livingston
__HP706	*The Dwelling Place*, K. Miller
__HP709	*That Wilder Boy*, K. V. Sawyer
__HP710	*To Love Again*, J. L. Barton
__HP713	*Secondhand Heart*, J. Livingston
__HP714	*Anna's Journey*, N. Toback
__HP717	*Merely Players*, K. Kovach
__HP718	*In His Will*, C. Hake
__HP721	*Through His Grace*, K. Hake
__HP722	*Christmas Mommy*, T. Fowler
__HP725	*By His Hand*, J. Johnson
__HP726	*Promising Angela*, K. V. Sawyer
__HP729	*Bay Hideaway*, B. Loughner
__HP730	*With Open Arms*, J. L. Barton
__HP733	*Safe in His Arms*, T. Davis
__HP734	*Larkspur Dreams*, A. Higman and J. A. Thompson
__HP737	*Darcy's Inheritance*, L. Ford
__HP738	*Picket Fence Pursuit*, J. Johnson
__HP741	*The Heart of the Matter*, K. Dykes
__HP742	*Prescription for Love*, A. Boeshaar
__HP745	*Family Reunion*, J. L. Barton
__HP746	*By Love Acquitted*, Y. Lehman
__HP749	*Love by the Yard*, G. Sattler
__HP750	*Except for Grace*, T. Fowler
__HP753	*Long Trail to Love*, P. Griffin
__HP754	*Red Like Crimson*, J. Thompson
__HP757	*Everlasting Love*, L. Ford
__HP758	*Wedded Bliss*, K. Y'Barbo
__HP761	*Double Blessing*, D. Mayne
__HP762	*Photo Op*, L. A. Coleman
__HP765	*Sweet Sugared Love*, P. Griffin
__HP766	*Pursuing the Goal*, J. Johnson
__HP769	*Who Am I?*, L. N. Dooley
__HP770	*And Baby Makes Five*, G. G. Martin
__HP773	*A Matter of Trust*, L. Harris
__HP774	*The Groom Wore Spurs*, J. Livingston
__HP777	*Seasons of Love*, E. Goddard
__HP778	*The Love Song*, J. Thompson
__HP781	*Always Yesterday*, J. Odell
__HP782	*Trespassed Hearts*, L. A. Coleman
__HP785	*If the Dress Fits*, D. Mayne
__HP786	*White as Snow*, J. Thompson

Great Inspirational Romance at a Great Price!

Heartsong Presents books are inspirational romances in contemporary and historical settings, designed to give you an enjoyable, spirit-lifting reading experience. You can choose wonderfully written titles from some of today's best authors like Wanda E. Brunstetter, Mary Connealy, Susan Page Davis, Cathy Marie Hake, Joyce Livingston, and many others.

When ordering quantities less than twelve, above titles are $2.97 each.
Not all titles may be available at time of order.

SEND TO: **Heartsong Presents** Readers' Service
P.O. Box 721, Uhrichsville, Ohio 44683

Please send me the items checked above. I am enclosing $ _____
(please add $3.00 to cover postage per order. OH add 7% tax. WA add 8.5%). Send check or money order, no cash or C.O.D.s, please.
To place a credit card order, call 1-740-922-7280.

NAME _____

ADDRESS _____

CITY/STATE _____ ZIP _____

HEARTSONG PRESENTS

If you love Christian romance...

$10.⁹⁹

You'll love Heartsong Presents' inspiring and faith-filled romances by today's very best Christian authors. . .Wanda E. Brunstetter, Mary Connealy, Susan Page Davis, Cathy Marie Hake, and Joyce Livingston, to mention a few!

When you join Heartsong Presents, you'll enjoy four brand-new, mass market, 176-page books—two contemporary and two historical—that will build you up in your faith when you discover God's role in every relationship you read about!

Imagine. . .four new romances every four weeks—with men and women like you who long to meet the one God has chosen as the love of their lives…all for the low price of $10.99 postpaid.

Mass Market 176 Pages

To join, simply visit www.heartsong presents.com or complete the coupon below and mail it to the address provided.

YES! Sign me up for Heartsong!

NEW MEMBERSHIPS WILL BE SHIPPED IMMEDIATELY!
Send no money now. We'll bill you only $10.99 postpaid with your first shipment of four books. Or for faster action, call 1-740-922-7280.

NAME_____

ADDRESS_____

CITY_____ STATE _____ ZIP _____

MAIL TO: HEARTSONG PRESENTS, P.O. Box 721, Uhrichsville, Ohio 44683
or sign up at WWW.HEARTSONGPRESENTS.COM